THE VALQUEZ
BRIDE

THE VALQUEZ BRIDE

BY
MELANIE MILBURNE

First published in Great Britain 2014
by Mills & Boon, an imprint of Harlequin (UK) Limited,
Large Print edition 2015
Eton House, 18-24 Paradise Road,
Richmond, Surrey, TW9 1SR

© 2014 Melanie Milburne

ISBN: 978-0-263-25596-6

Harlequin (UK) Limited's policy is to use papers that are natural, renewable and recyclable products and made from wood grown in sustainable forests. The logging and manufacturing processes conform to the legal environmental regulations of the country of origin.

Printed and bound in Great Britain
by CPI Antony Rowe, Chippenham, Wiltshire

To Nataly Espinoza,
for your help with the Spanish translations,
but also for your friendship.
It was lovely meeting you
on the tour of The Kimberleys. xxx

CHAPTER ONE

THE ONE WORD that stood out on Teddy's father's will started with M but it wasn't money. She looked at the family lawyer in open-mouthed alarm. '*Marriage?*'

Benson nodded gravely. 'I'm afraid so. Within a month. Otherwise, your second cousin Hugo will inherit the lot—every property, stock and share, including Marlstone Manor.'

'But that can't be right!' Teddy gripped the arms of the chair so tightly her fingers dug into the leather arms like claws. 'Dad told me this place was mine. He told me the day before he died. He said I would *always* have this roof over my head.'

'Your father changed his will the month before he was diagnosed with cancer,' the lawyer said. 'It was as if he'd known he didn't have much time left and wanted to get his affairs in order.'

His affairs?

It was *her* home! That was *her* affair. It was *her* life! It was her safety and security. How could her father hand it over to her cousin, who hadn't even visited him once during his illness?

Teddy's heart was galloping so fast and so hard she could feel the blood beating in every one of her fingertips. Shock chilled and chugged through her body like a flow of ice. She blinked to clear her vision. What sort of nightmare was this? Was she really sitting in the library with her father's lawyer having this crazy conversation?

It had to be a mistake.

For the last five months she had nursed her father through his pancreatic cancer and stayed with him and held his hand as he finally slipped away. It was the only time she had felt close to him. During those last days he had shared snippets of his childhood previously unknown to her. It had explained so much about his difficult personality. The way he had constantly found fault with her. How he was so impossible to please. How he was such a control freak who never let her have a say in things. Towards the end she had found a space in her heart to forgive him. She had even told him she loved him. Something she had vowed she would never do.

And yet the whole time he had been intent on tricking her?

Betraying her?

She swallowed tightly, annoyed at the knotty lump of hurt that was lodged in her throat like an oversized walnut. Why had she fallen for it? Why had she let her father *do* that to her? He had made her feel safe and then whipped the rug of security out from under her. Why hadn't she seen it coming? Why had she been so...so *stupid* to fall for that happy families routine?

'My father led me to believe Marlstone would always be mine.' Teddy tried to speak clearly and steadily even though her emotions were tumbling and twisting inside her chest like clothes spinning in a dryer set on too fast a speed. 'Why would he have changed his mind? Surely I don't have to be married in order to inherit what should be automatically mine? That's totally outrageous!'

The lawyer tapped the legal document with the pen he was holding. 'It's a little more specific than that...' He paused for a beat as if he was trying to find a way to say his next words without causing her more stress. 'Your father has also nominated the groom.'

Shock opened a broad hand inside her belly and grabbed at her intestines. Nominated the—*'What?'*

He pushed the document towards her. 'He wants you to marry Alejandro Valquez.'

Teddy looked at the name. Saw the man in her mind. Felt the bottom of her spine loosen as she pictured that imposingly tall, dark-haired, dark-eyed playboy with the enigmatic smile of a fallen angel. The man women the world over flocked around like bees to top shelf pollen. She felt her cheeks heat up as if twin furnaces had been lit beneath her skin. This had to be a joke. Her father couldn't possibly be so cruel. To force her to marry someone so out of her league it would make her a laughing stock the moment it was announced. The press would mock her. They would ridicule her mercilessly. No one would believe it for a second. Alejandro Valquez and *her?* She could already see the headlines: *Lame Lady of the Manor Lands Argentinian Playboy in Money Match Marriage.*

What had she done to deserve this? Was this her father's way of showing his disgust for her disability? To make her a target of ridicule and derision? To be the butt of puerile bar room jokes for the next decade?

Teddy took a steadying breath, slowly bringing her gaze back up to the lawyer's. She had to keep cool. There had to be a way to solve this. It wasn't going to help things by panicking and getting hysterical. That wasn't her way. Cool and composed was her modus operandi, even though below the surface her nerves were stretched to snapping point. 'Is there any way of…getting around it?'

'Not if you want to retain full ownership and occupancy of Marlstone Manor.'

She looked out of the library windows to the gardens and the rolling fields beyond. The green folded valleys with their borders of thick hedgerows, the curve of the river that flowed through the forest that fringed the upper boundary. The still and silent silver sheet of the lake, the sycamore, beech and yew trees that had stood for centuries while life moved on around them.

The Wiltshire mansion and its surrounding estate was her home. It was her inspiration for her work as a children's book illustrator. Her botanical drawings with their whimsical themes were inspired by her surroundings.

Her studio was here.

Her home was here.

Her sanctuary was here.

How could she lose it? How could she be turfed out as if she was nothing more than a leaseholder? What was her father thinking?

Her stomach knotted again.

Hadn't he cared about her at all?

Hadn't he known how much she loathed men like Alejandro Valquez? Alejandro was a disgustingly rich and dashingly handsome playboy who—like his younger brother Luiz—only ever dated supermodels and film stars. Beautiful women. Perfect women.

Alejandro hadn't noticed her in the past. Girls

like her were invisible to men like him. His coal-black gaze had looked straight through her when he'd been introduced to her at a polo event her father had taken her to years ago.

Alejandro had barely mouthed a word of greeting before he had spied a tall, slim blonde beauty standing behind her, who soon after became his fiancée. Their whirlwind affair had been in the press for weeks—for months—until his fiancée, supermodel Mercedes Delgado, called off their wedding at the last minute.

What was her father playing at in forcing the hand of a man who could choose any woman he liked? What possible reason could her father have for wanting such an alliance, even if it was only temporary?

Teddy had never been close to her father. He had never disguised the fact he would have preferred a son to a daughter. Since her childhood he had found fault with her for everything she said or did, and yet, like all little girls, she had continued to love him. To seek his approval. To win him over. It had taken her years to realise he had been too obsessed with work and winning every corporate battle to care about her. He hadn't had time for her, even though he had gone to extreme lengths to secure custody of her after the divorce from her mother. Gaining custody of her had been another battle to win. Another victory.

Was this his way of punishing her for never forgiving him for the way he had driven her mother to an early grave? Or had he been so ashamed of his only daughter living such a quiet spinsterish life he had decided to do something about it by tying her to a man she had no possible chance of attracting any other way?

The Valquez name was synonymous with wealth and prestige. The playboy polo set who partied as hard as they played. If and when the fast-living brothers decided to marry, it certainly wouldn't be to someone like her.

Teddy brought her gaze back to the lawyer's. 'What's in this for Alejandro? Why would he agree to such an arrangement?'

'Your father bought some acreage off Alejandro's father in Argentina twenty years ago to relieve financial pressure on the family after Paco

Valquez suffered a polo accident and became a quadriplegic,' Benson said. 'Your father kept it in his possession all this time, even though Alejandro has made numerous offers to buy it back. The deeds of the property will be handed over to him upon your marriage.'

She was being exchanged for property? Handed over like a trophy? Like goods and chattels? How could her father do this to her? This wasn't the Regency period. This was the twenty-first century. Women were supposed to choose their own husbands.

To fall in love.

To be loved back.

Teddy had secretly dreamed of having the fairy tale since her parents divorced so acrimoniously when she was seven. She believed in the power of love even though she hadn't seen it modelled or experienced it herself. People were supposed to fall in love and stay in love. Not marry each other for prestige or property or financial gain.

How could she ignore the deepest yearnings of her heart to marry for any other reason than love? It would compromise every value she held dear. She refused to turn into a version of her mother, marrying a man for the social status and security he could give her and then suffering the shame of having everyone laugh at her when it all came unstuck.

There *had* to be a way out of this.

Teddy looked at the lawyer again. 'What does Alejandro think about this? Has he been told?'

'He is in what I would describe as rather a bind,' the lawyer said.

'Meaning?'

'Your father has set things up so that if Alejandro refuses to marry you the property he wants will be sold.'

'But surely a man with his sort of wealth could buy it when it goes on the market?'

The lawyer shook his head. 'I'm afraid that is not possible. Your father has strictly stated that the property will be sold to a developer if Alejandro refuses to comply with the terms of the will. A local developer has already shown some interest and will snap up the property in a heartbeat as soon as it's released. I would imagine Alejandro wouldn't relinquish that land lightly, even if it meant marrying a perfect stranger. Looking at it like that, it's a win-win for both of you.'

Teddy's bile rose like frothing acid. Did her father's lawyer—like everyone else—think she had no hope of finding a husband any other way? She pulled her shoulders back and gave the lawyer one of her trademark arctic looks. 'You can tell Señor Valquez there is no possible circumstance I can think of where I would ever agree to marry him.'

'Are you kidding me?' Alejandro glared at the legal representative from Marlstone Incorporated in his London office.

'If you want the Mendoza land Clark Marlstone bought off your father, then that's what you have to do.'

'He didn't buy it off my father,' Alejandro said through clenched teeth, 'he *stole* it. He paid a fraction of what it was worth. He took advantage of my father's financial situation after the accident. He manipulated things so he could get his hands on that land while making everyone think he was doing us a favour.' *Bastard.*

'Be that as it may, you have a chance to get it back without having to pay a single peso for it.'

Alejandro sucked in a lungful of air through his nostrils. He would have to pay for it all right. With his freedom. The thing he valued above all else. 'I don't even remember meeting Marlstone's daughter.' He glanced at the name and frowned. 'Theodora, is it? Who is she? What's she got to say about this, or is she the one behind it?'

He could already picture her. Pampered and spoilt. Another cheap little gold-digger wanting to marry up. A social climbing daddy's girl who wanted her life made easy. He could just imagine how she had talked her ailing father into engineering things so she would be home free. Married to a rich trophy husband, all without having to bat a coquettish eyelid.

Not on his watch, damn it.

'She's as annoyed as you are,' his lawyer said. 'She intends to contest the will.'

As if. Alejandro knew the way women played

all too well. Theodora Marlstone would protest and make a fuss for show. To put him off the scent of her avaricious motives. Of course she'd want to marry him. He was considered a Prize Catch. One of the most eligible bachelors in Argentina, if not the entire world. 'What are her chances?'

'Not good,' the lawyer said. 'The will is iron-clad. Clark Marlstone wrote it while of sound mind. He got three doctors to confirm it, one imagines because he suspected one or both of you would resist his instructions and try and find a loophole. It would be a costly and lengthy exercise to try and overturn it. My advice is to do what it says and make the best of it. It's only for six months.'

Easy for you to say.

Alejandro ploughed a hand through his hair. He already had too many responsibilities with his fostering of two street kids, Sofi and Jorge, providing food, shelter, education and a sense of family for them, or at least as far as it was possible for a bachelor to do. He didn't need a wife to add to his troubles. Fifteen-year-old Jorge was still in that tricky stage of deciding whether to rebel or respect authority, reminding him of his younger brother Luiz at that age and the lengths he'd had to go to and the sacrifices he'd had to make to keep him from harm. While eighteen-year-old Sofi was a little more mature, she had recently expressed a desire to move to Buenos Aires to study hair and beauty. He wasn't completely comfortable with the idea of her living in the big city without the close support he and the rest of his household staff provided for her.

Marrying would be a hard enough decision to make if he cared about someone enough to consider that sort of commitment. But how was he supposed to marry a perfect stranger? He felt antsy at the thought of marriage. Of being tied down. Of allowing someone the power to be there one minute and not there the next. Like his mother had been for his father. Proudly wearing his ring and rearing his sons one minute, bolting out of the gate to a new life in France, leaving the ring and divorce papers and two bewildered little boys behind the next.

Alejandro had tried commitment once and it

had failed. Spectacularly. Even worse, he hadn't seen it coming. It annoyed him that he had let what he *felt* block out what he *knew.* In his experience women wanted one thing and he'd been foolish to think otherwise. They wanted money and security. They did anything they could to get it. They fell in love and out of love according to the size of a man's wallet. He didn't care if it was hardwired into their primitive DNA. He would not be manipulated, cajoled, tricked into falling for it again.

He was older and smarter now. He never let his feelings get in the way of a good business deal. He never let his feelings cloud his judgement, colour his thinking or distract him from a task. He hadn't rebuilt his father's failing empire by *feeling.* He had done it by blood and sweat and outsmarting the opposition. Whatever roadblocks were put in front of him he stepped over, circumvented. Obliterated.

This would be no different.

'Where is she?' Alejandro asked the immaculately dressed and imperious-looking butler who answered the door at Marlstone Manor in Wiltshire.

Bushy brows as white and hairy as two caterpillars gave an austere frown over rheumy blue eyes. 'Miss Teddy is currently engaged.'

Now *that* was funny. If only she were engaged. To someone else.

'I'm sure she'll shoehorn me into her busy schedule.' He suppressed a cynical snort. Miss Theodora Marlstone was probably waiting for her spray tan to dry, or her nail polish, or curling her eyelash extensions or some such nonsense. Could there be any woman more vacuous than a pampered daddy's girl?

And what the hell sort of name was Teddy? What did she think she was—a toy or a person?

'If you will kindly wait here I will tell her you have requested an interview with—'

'Look, no offence, buddy,' Alejandro cut in, 'but I haven't got the time or the inclination to hang around and wait for your mistress to glue her fake nails on. You either lead me to her or I go looking for her. Which is it to be?'

'Neither,' a cool voice said from behind him.

Alejandro turned to see a small figure standing in the frame of the doorway off the black and white tiled hall. There wasn't a fake nail in sight or a spray tan. She was wearing clothes that looked as if they had been sourced from a charity bin and her hair looked as if she had dived in head first to retrieve them. It was a wild cloud of dark brown tresses around her head and shoulders, wavy rather than curly, but clearly no effort had been spared to tame it. If anything, it looked as if she had recently mussed it up with her hands. Her trousers were a dirty shade of brown, the checked shirt unironed, and the cable sweater she wore over it was covered in balls of lint. The outfit was masculine and too big for her small frame, swamping her like a tent draped over a toothpick.

Why on earth had she dressed in such an appalling manner? What was she trying to prove? The girl was an heiress to a spectacular estate worth millions. She could afford to wear the best of high street fashion. Why was she dressing like a bag lady?

His eyes went to the bone-handled walking

stick she was leaning on in what he could only describe as a proudly defiant manner.

He felt something jerk in his chest like a foot did when it missed a step.

So that was why.

'Miss Marlstone?'

'Señor Valquez, how nice to see you again.'

Alejandro didn't like the feeling of being at a disadvantage. Of her knowing more about him than he knew about her. Keep your friends close and your enemies closer was a credo he lived by. And yet there was something about her that appealed to the protector in him. 'We've…er… met before?'

She gave him a stiff movement of her lips that passed for a smile but he noticed it didn't involve her arctic-cool grey-blue eyes. 'Yes.' Her chin rose ever so slightly. 'Don't you remember?'

Alejandro quickly checked his mental hard drive. He dated a lot of women. Slept with even more. But nowhere in his memory could he find a girl with eyes so deeply set they looked darker than they actually were. She had prominent eyebrows and lashes thick and dark without the boost of mascara. Cheeks sharply defined and haughtily high and a nose that looked as if it spent a lot of time up there with them. A mouth that was full and young and innocent-looking and yet with an angle of cynicism to it that matched his own.

'I'm afraid you'll have to remind me.' He stretched his own lips into a half-mast smile. 'I meet a lot of people in my line of business.'

Her eyes were unnervingly steady as they held his. It was as if she were seeing past his urbane man-in-control-of-his-universe façade to the shy boy of ten who'd had to step up to the plate after his father's accident and his mother's desertion. Her face was free of make-up. No mask of cosmetics to hide behind and yet he couldn't help feeling she was a little too composed.

'We met at British Polo Day some years ago.'

'We did?'

'It was the same event where you met your ex-fiancée.'

Alejandro clenched his jaw behind his polite smile. She had gone for the jugular. *Bitch*. Like father, like daughter. Playing games with him. Toying with him. Mocking him.

Reminding him.

He hated being reminded of his foolishness back then. At twenty-four he had stupidly believed love existed. Back then he had believed he could have a happy and fulfilling life with someone who loved him as much as he loved them. That how much money he had or didn't have wouldn't count. He had been swept away by the notion of building a new family like the one his mother had destroyed when she'd left his shattered father six months after the accident.

He had been wrong.

'I'm sorry I have no recollection of our meeting.' He ran his gaze over her as he tried to judge her age. She looked to be in her early to mid-twenties but, without make-up and wearing those dreadful tomboy ragbag clothes, she looked far younger. 'Were we formally introduced?'

'Yes.'

Alejandro still couldn't place her. But then he met a lot of people during polo events. His brother played on the field while he worked the business end of things. Sponsors and corporate kings often pushed their daughters under his nose but he was always careful to keep business and pleasure separate. She had obviously taken it as a slight that he hadn't singled her out in the past. But then why would he? She was as far away from his usual type as could be. 'You must have been quite young at the time.'

'Sixteen.'

So that made her twenty-six now. A plain Jane single woman sliding down the slippery slope to the big three-oh, so Daddy had agreed to set her up with a mail order groom.

Alejandro's gut curdled with bitterness. Why had she chosen him? Why not some other guy who could stomach the thought of matrimony? Or was this some sort of payback for snubbing her in the past?

'Is there somewhere we could talk?' He threw a glance at the hovering butler, who looked as if he'd just stepped off a film shoot on a period drama. 'In private?'

'This way.'

Alejandro frowned as he followed her. She had

a pronounced limp that made the action of walking look not only awkward but also painful, in spite of the use of the stick. One leg dragged slightly as if the muscles weren't strong enough to take her full weight. Not that she was heavy or anything. She looked as if a gust of wind would send her into the next county. Was it a recent injury? He tried to recall if he had read anything about her in the press but he came up with zero. Perhaps she wasn't the press magnet type.

He felt a flicker of interest spark and fire in his brain. Not in-your-face beautiful and broken too. *Interesting.* Was this why she was being packaged in the marriage deal? Did she or her father—or both—think she couldn't get a husband any other way? She might not be billboard stunning but he could see the classical lines to her face, the porcelain skin that looked as soft and smooth and creamy as a magnolia petal, the unusual colour of her eyes that made him think of a winter lake. She had a quiet beauty that sneaked up on you without you noticing. It was the sort of beauty that would suddenly appear and snatch your breath.

She turned and faced him once they were in the library. Her expression was masked, like a puppet face that hadn't been animated. 'Would you care for a drink?'

'What happened to your leg?'

She pinched her lips together, pride flashing across her features as fast as the flick of a whip-lash. 'I have whisky or brandy or cognac. Wine too. Red. White. Champagne.'

'I asked you a question.'

Her eyes clashed with his, the chips of blue in hers striking in amongst the sea of grey. 'A rude one.'

Alejandro gave a careless shrug. He didn't care if he was rude. He wasn't here to make friends. He was here to get out of the stranglehold of her father's machinations. He wanted that land. He would do anything for that land.

But not this.

Not the *M* word.

He nailed her with a hardened look. 'I'm not here to drink wine and talk about the weather. I'm here to put a stop to this nonsense.'

Her expression remained composed. Determined. Implacable. 'I'm not marrying you.'

'Damn right you're not.'

'I have no intention of marrying anyone.'

'Couldn't agree more.'

'Which brings us to the rather vexing terms of my father's will.'

Vexing? Was she stuck in a time warp or something? She talked as if she had stepped out of the pages of a Brontë sister's novel.

Alejandro watched as she poured herself a glass of soda water. The silence was so intense he could hear the bubbles spitting and fizzing against the sides of the glass.

She had delicate hands, slim and long-fingered and milky-white like the rest of her skin. Her nails were short but not manicured that way. They were bitten down to the quick, one of them looking red and painful near the cuticle.

With her awful clothes and the absence of make-up and any other adornment such as jewellery, he suspected it had been a deliberate choice to make herself as unattractive as possible. Intriguing thought. Why would she do that? She stood to gain the most out of this deal. Or lose the most. Her inheritance rested on her agreement to the terms. A distant relative would get everything if she didn't comply with her father's wishes. What young woman would turn her back on an inheritance worth several millions? Marlstone Manor and its surrounding estate was a property developer's dream. And then there was her father's investment and property portfolio that would leave her without money worries for the rest of her life.

He studied her for another beat or two before he asked, 'You didn't know he'd planned things this way?'

'No.'

She had the amazing ability to say a lot with one word, Alejandro thought. She could communicate an entire library of words with a look. And right now she was looking at him as if he had come into her neat-as-a-pin sitting room with his back hunched and his knuckles dragging.

He wasn't used to women despising him on sight. He was used to women fawning over him and worshipping him. It came with the territory of Having Money. Everyone loved money. Especially women. It opened more bedroom doors than anything else.

He found her ice maiden approach refreshing. Delightfully entertaining. He hadn't felt this level of interest in a long time, if ever. He could feel the little tick in his blood. The tempo raising just enough to make him aware of the physical needs he had been neglecting of late, due to the pressure of juggling work and his responsibilities at home. There was nothing he liked more than a challenge—the harder the quest the better. It made claiming the victory all the more satisfying.

He knew he could have her if he made a play for her. He could have any woman he wanted. Vanity had nothing to do with it. He could look as ugly as sin and he would still be able to draw a woman into his sensual web.

Ever since his broken engagement he had made it his business to select and seduce. He never stayed with a lover more than a couple of weeks. He was a sexual grazer. He took what was on offer and moved on before expectations made things messy.

'What do you plan to do about this…er…vexing situation we find ourselves in?' he said.

Her chin was thrust at a pugnacious height, her eyes glittering with such defiance and spirit he felt a tingling sensation at the base of his spine. 'I'm seeking legal advice.'

'Good luck with that.'

Her forehead puckered. 'What's that supposed to mean?'

Alejandro wandered over to the bookshelves to see what her taste was in reading. All the classics were there. No surprise. There was a scattering of modern works, mostly thrillers and adventure and a larger selection of romance. Interesting. Did Miss Uptight Teddy Marlstone have a secret desire to be wooed and won?

'I said, what's that supposed to mean?'

He smiled as he pushed the spine of the book he'd inspected back in alignment with the others. Now he was getting somewhere. Getting under that starchy façade to see who she really was when she wasn't trying to be a pain in the butt. He slowly turned and ran his gaze over her assessingly. 'In my experience, lawyers drive expensive cars paid for by their clients.'

Her throat moved up and down like a small creature under a rug, the only crack so far in her cool composure. 'So?'

'Are you sure you can afford it?'

Two spots of rosy pink stained her cheeks but her gaze was as caustic as ever. 'I haven't sponged off my father, if that's what you're implying. I have my own source of income.'

'As a children's book illustrator, right?'

'That's correct.'

'I've never seen any of your work.'

Her eyes pulsated with dislike. 'I can assure you I'm quite popular with whom it counts.'

Alejandro suppressed a smile. He was enjoying their verbal stoush much more than he'd expected to. She was prim and proper and yet fiercely proud. He liked someone who could stand up for what they believed in. Who wasn't intimidated or put off by others' egos or agendas. She wasn't fazed by him or by his reputation. She was making no attempt to disguise her dislike of him. He liked that. He liked it a lot. 'We have a month to decide what to do.'

Her chin came up again and stayed up. 'I have already decided.'

So had he…or so he'd thought.

Maybe a short-term marriage on paper would be worth considering after all.

He *wanted* that land.

It was a thousand hectares of prime real estate that had been in his family for generations, and would still have been except for Teddy's father's underhand dealings. Alejandro's plans to extend his polo pony-breeding stud with an exclusive resort attached couldn't go ahead without that land. It was perfectly positioned, with good grazing and access, and wouldn't interfere or compromise the rest of his estate. Sustainable farming was an important issue to him and without that land being returned to his possession he couldn't rest easy that it would be taken care of in the best way possible. What if Teddy's relative sold it to a developer? There were plenty about, looking for properties to exploit. The place would be desecrated and his along with it. He had to stop that happening. He would do anything to stop that happening.

Almost anything.

'Are you really prepared to throw all of this away?' He waved a hand to encompass her gracious surroundings.

She eyeballed him with that same piercing intensity. 'Are you really prepared to marry a perfect stranger in exchange for a plot of land?'

He sent his gaze over her in a long lazy sweep, taking in the swell of her small pert breasts the voluminous sweater couldn't quite conceal. 'I'm thinking about it.'

Her eyes flickered and then widened as if she couldn't quite believe her ears.

Alejandro was with her on that. He couldn't believe his either. Had he really just said he was *thinking* about it? Red flag. Panic button. Exit stage left.

He was thinking about the M word?

'Why is the land of such importance to you?' she asked.

The one thing Alejandro had learned in business was not to show how much you wanted something. It gave the opposition too much power. It was better to act cool and indifferent, as if this was just another business transaction. Nothing out of the ordinary. Easy come, easy go.

'The land is not the issue. The issue is whether I would feel comfortable watching you lose everything for the sake of six months in a paper marriage.'

Her throat rose and fell again as she made a little gulping sound. 'Did you say…*paper*?'

CHAPTER TWO

'BUT OF COURSE.' Alejandro hooked a pitch-black eyebrow upwards. 'You surely weren't expecting anything else?'

Teddy tried to read his glinting expression. Was he mocking her or baiting her?

It didn't take her long to decide. He was mocking her. *Bastard.* Did he have to make it so plainly obvious she was not his type? *Grr.* She had deliberately made herself look as unappealing as possible when she'd seen his top end sports car prowl up the long driveway. Well, even *more* unappealing given her damaged hip was no doubt the biggest turn-off for a man who only dated long-legged blondes.

The arrogance of him! He hadn't even called first to make an appointment to see her. What sort of person *did* that? What did he think she did all day? Swan around the manor with a champagne cocktail in her hand?

How hard would it have been to call and make a time? What right did he have to come barging in *demanding* she see him? Did he think she was hanging out here with her heart all aflutter, waiting for him to turn up and dash her off to the nearest register office?

If so, he had better think again. She was determined to show him she wasn't one of his brainless bimbos who drooled at the mere sight of him.

He might be quite possibly the most gorgeous-looking man she had ever seen, even more gorgeous than those hot male models who advertised aftershave or designer brand sunglasses. He might have the most amazingly dark brown eyes that made her think of strong espresso coffee, and a mouth that made her think of sex, which was a little bit shocking because she *never* thought of sex. He might have a body that would make Michelangelo make a dash for the nearest chisel and a block of marble, but *she* was not going to be swooning or fainting any time soon.

No way.

She was going to show him he couldn't just waltz into her house and tell her how high to jump.

Firstly, she couldn't jump.

And secondly…well, a girl had her pride, didn't she? She didn't want to be handed over like a raffle prize. He didn't want *her*. He wanted the land his father had sold to her father. He wanted it more than he was letting on.

That was the thing about being a wallflower. Teddy got to stand back and observe people. To see all the nuances that gave them away. He was better than most at keeping his cards concealed, but she knew he was a powerful and ruthlessly dangerous opponent. He had a winner takes all aura about him. He wore arrogance as easily as he wore his bespoke clothes. He would take risks but only if he was absolutely certain they would pay off. He was calculating and cool. Clever and far more attractive than any man had a right to be. Impressively tall, six-foot-four, and olive-skinned, with jet-black hair that was styled in a casually tousled way—not too short, not too long, but somewhere fashionably in between. His uncompromising jaw was lean and shaven but the regrowth that currently shadowed it suggested he was a twice a day shaver.

Somehow the thought of the rush of those male hormones surging through his body made her insides shift. She was aware of him in a way she didn't want to own. Would *not* show. He was used to reeling in women like the catch of the day. He pulled them in and then tossed them away when he was done with them. She wasn't going to be lured in by his potent charm and undoubted sensual expertise.

No-ho-ho way.

'Señor Valquez, you seem to have the misguided notion that I am agreeable to any sort of marriage with you. I hate to slight your undoubtedly robust ego, but that is not the case.'

The right side of his mouth came up in an arrogant tilt, those bedroom eyes glinting so darkly the lining of her belly gave an involuntary quiver. 'You have a lot to lose by rejecting my offer of a temporary marriage.'

Teddy kept her gaze trained on his. 'So, it seems, do you.'

The only sign of his tension was in a muscle that moved near the left side of his jaw. It was barely more than a flicker but it told her much more about him than anything he had said so far.

He didn't want to marry her any more than she wanted to marry him. He was playing a game. Getting control. He was ruthlessly determined. Powerfully motivated. He would do whatever it took to get what he wanted and he wouldn't care who got hurt in the process.

The air tightened like a singing wire.

Sparks passed from his gaze to hers. She felt the impact of them as if he had fired a laser at her. It was all she could do not to blink. It was all she could do not to stare at his mouth. Had she ever seen such a masculine mouth? Such a *beautiful* mouth? That was the only word to describe it. It was like a work of art. Sexy and sensually contoured with its surround of dark stubble. A tempting mouth. A sinfully corrupt mouth. A mouth that took what it wanted because it damn well could.

Something deep and low in her belly got out of its tightly locked cage. It stretched its cramped limbs, started to move, to crawl around inside her, stirring her senses into wakefulness. It sent a tremor through her blood like a shockwave through a millpond. She could feel the tiny ripples moving over her flesh like the spread of a shiver.

His gaze drifted to her mouth, lingering there for a pulsing beat before re-engaging with her gaze with a zap she felt deep in her core. 'I'll give you twenty-four hours to make up your mind. After that the offer is off the table and a new one will take its place.'

Teddy worked hard to keep her expression masked. What other offer would he present to her? Dared she ask? His coal-black eyes were locked on hers in a silent challenge that made the air vibrate with soundless waves of antagonism. The back of her neck prickled as every tiny hair stood to attention like soldiers under the threat of enemy fire. She drew in a breath but the space inside her chest felt cramped, as if her ribcage was slowly but surely shrinking back against her

spine. 'You seem assured I will eventually ca-
pitulate to your wishes, Señor Valquez. Again,
I would hate to unnecessarily damage your ego
but I will not be told what to do.'

His slant of a smile ignited a satirical glint in
his eyes. 'It's your call, Miss Marlstone. Today
it's a marriage on paper. This time tomorrow it
will be the real deal.' He handed her a business
card with his contact details on it. 'Let me know
which you decide.'

Teddy took the card because she didn't know
what else to do. She couldn't get her voice to
work. Couldn't get her brain to think. Couldn't
stop her body from feeling hot all over from the
smouldering burn of his gaze.

Was he serious? Was he prepared to go *that*
far? To make it a real marriage in every sense
of the word?

To her?

Why would he do that? Why would he want
that? Why would he want *her*? Or was he game
playing, to see how far he could push her?

Teddy watched as he strode out of the door.
Listened to him speak curtly with Henry, the

butler, on his way out. Heard the front door click shut on his exit. Heard the roar of his powerful engine and the spin of his tyres on the gravel of the driveway as he sped away, throwing up a shower of stones that hit the side of the house like a spray of bullets.

She closed her hand over the business card and felt the edges bite into the flesh of her palm. It was a chilling reminder that in any further skirmish with him she would have to be better prepared. Armoured up. Invincible.

And she only had twenty-four hours in which to do it….

'If you ask me, I think you'd be crazy not to marry him,' Audrey, the long-time housekeeper said as she poked a blue delphinium into the arrangement she was making in the kitchen. 'After all, what's going to happen to all of our jobs if this place is handed over to your layabout cousin? He won't keep Henry on at his age, not to mention me.' She gave a little sniff as she picked up another bloom. 'He'll want some big-breasted young floozy to flounce around the place with a feather duster in her hand before she dives into his bed.'

Teddy chewed at her lip. She hadn't got as far as thinking about the loyal Marlstone staff. They were a team. A family. *Her family.* Audrey Taylor was sixty-eight and had run the household ever since Teddy's mother had left. She had fulfilled so many roles in Teddy's life: nanny, friend, confidante, wise counsel and mentor.

Seventy-four-year-old Henry Buckington had worked for her father's father before her parents were married. He was part of the furniture. The place wouldn't be the same without his stolid presence.

Then there was Stan and Myles Harris, the father and son team who managed the garden and the rest of the estate.

Audrey was right. Teddy's cousin would bring in his own staff, not keep the ones who had served her and her father so loyally for so long. They would be cast out and left to flounder.

But could she marry a man she didn't know to save them? A man she didn't even like? A man she detested for his cocksure arrogance?

Alejandro Valquez expected her to say yes. Any other woman would have said yes ten times over. That's what was so galling. He expected her to feel *grateful* that he was so magnanimously offering his hand in marriage.

A *paper* marriage.

How insulting was that? Could he make it any more obvious he thought her a deformed freak? *Of course* he would offer her a paper marriage. What else? He wouldn't want her in his bed… not that she *wanted* to be in his bed or anything. A girl might have the odd erotic fantasy, which was perfectly natural, but it didn't *mean* anything. It wasn't as if she was hankering after a red-hot affair with him just because he was so staggeringly handsome…but still.

'Did you know Dad had written his will like this?'

Audrey snipped off the end of the stalk of the flower she was holding. 'I suspected he might.'

Teddy frowned. 'You did? Why?' *Why didn't you think to mention it during the last five months while I nursed him and stupidly fooled myself into believing he cared about me?*

The housekeeper put down the secateurs and gave Teddy a direct look. 'You don't need me to tell you your father was a stubborn old goat who thought his way was the only way. I expect he was worried about you being left on your own. This is a big estate for a young woman to run without a husband by her side.'

'So he engineered one for me? Do you know how…how *insulting* that is?' Teddy folded her arms. 'I can find my own husband, thanks very much.'

Audrey's gaze had a wise old owl look about it. 'You'd better get a wriggle on, lass. You're not getting any younger.'

'For God's sake, I'm only twenty-six.'

Four years until she was thirty. Was that the sound of ticking she could hear? When she was a little girl she thought she would be married with a baby by now. As a little girl she had dressed up in her mother's exquisite wedding gown and veil and tottered around in her high heels pretending to be a princess bride, dreaming of the day when she would become one for real. How far had life taken her away from her hopes and dreams? Her riding accident when she was ten had changed everything. She had gone from being normal to disabled. To being on the outside of everything. The odd one out. The poor little lame girl. The girl no one wanted on their team.

The girl no one wanted unless they could be bribed or bought.

'Yes, but you haven't been on a date since you came home from art school.' Audrey picked up the secateurs and another bloom. Snip. Snip. Snip.

Teddy pressed her lips together. 'I'm not good at dating.'

Audrey cocked her head as she studied the floral arrangement. 'You don't try, that's why.'

Teddy frowned again. 'I'm not a party girl. I never have been. I hate small talk. I'd rather paint or read a book.'

'Alejandro Valquez has plenty of friends. Maybe he can lend you some.'

'Oh, yes, I can just imagine me becoming chummy with all his pretty pin-up girls.' She narrowed her gaze at the housekeeper. 'Anyway, why are you so for this crazy scheme?'

Audrey gave her a pragmatic look. 'I don't want you to lose your home and this is the only way you can keep it. Your father was old-fashioned and set in his ways. He wanted to see you settled. He wanted you to marry a man of means. I suspect he thought this was the best way to do it.'

'It's the worst possible way!' Teddy said. 'I haven't got a say in it. It's being forced on me.'

'I expect it's the same for Alejandro.'

'No, it's not.' Teddy balled her fists and set her jaw. 'It's not the same at all. He thinks it's amusing to stride into my life and tell me what to do as if I have no mind or will of my own. I loathe him. He's insufferably rude and arrogant. He thinks I'm gagging to say yes to him.' *Argh!*

'He's one of the richest men in Argentina.'

'If he's so rich then why's he so worried about a plot of land he could buy a squillion times over?'

'It's adjacent to his family property, that's why,' Audrey said. 'I expect he can't expand his polo breeding stud without it. He rebuilt his father's polo resort business from scratch. He took over as CEO when he was in his early twenties. He's been trying to get that land back ever since.'

Teddy rolled her eyes. 'I suppose he wants to build some ghastly flashy hotel on it. What sort of man does that? Why doesn't he want to preserve it for future generations to enjoy?'

Audrey shrugged. 'Why don't you ask him when you call him?'

Teddy folded her arms again. 'I'm not calling him.'

'You have to call him to give him your answer.'

'My answer is no.'

Audrey let out a long whoosh of a sigh, her hunched shoulders going down with it. 'I guess I'd better start packing my things…'

'Oh, no you don't.' Teddy unfolded her arms to waggle a finger at her. 'Don't you go emotionally blackmailing me because it won't work.' *Much.*

Teddy hated the thought of her staff losing their home and their source of income. Their security. Their sense of purpose. It was giving her an ulcer just thinking about it. What would they do? Where would they go? What would happen to them? They weren't the sort of people who could sit around and do nothing. They loved working at Marlstone Manor. It kept them active and mentally stimulated.

Could she do what was necessary to rescue them? Could she marry a man in order to keep her family home secure? Could she make that sacrifice for the sake of the only people she thought of as family?

It was only for six months.

It was a paper marriage.

The time would be up before she knew it. It wasn't as if she had to move to Argentina with him. He wouldn't want the inconvenience of a wife living under his roof while he partied all night with his lady friends. Oh, no. He would want her safely ensconced back here in England. Out of sight, out of mind.

'You can't fight this, Teddy. You can't fight him.'

'Are you talking about Dad or Alejandro?'

Audrey gave her a speaking look. 'Both.'

* * *

'You're not seriously thinking of going through with it?' Luiz said when he called Alejandro.

'I want that land.'

'Heck of a way to go about it,' Luiz drawled. 'I thought you said you were never going to darken the doorstep of a church ever—'

'Yeah, well, this is different.'

Alejandro had thought it through from every angle. He would suffer the short-term marriage because it would achieve his long-term goal. It was a matter of honour. The land was Valquez land his forebears had owned for generations. Clark Marlstone had swindled Alejandro's father at a low point in his life and it was up to *him* to get it back.

To bring about justice.

So what if he had to marry the enemy's daughter to do it? It wasn't as if he were *really* marrying her. It would be a civil ceremony. He would not stand in a church and make promises he had no intention of keeping. He would continue to live his life the way he wanted to live it.

Teddy Marlstone would get what she wanted at the end.

So would he.

'It's only for six months,' he said. 'After that, I'll have the marriage annulled. By then we'll both have what we want.' Too easy.

'What's she like?'

Alejandro frowned as he thought of Teddy's marked limp. Had that had something to do with her father's machinations? Clark Marlstone was marrying her off because she was maimed? That was despicable but then it was just the sort of thing a man like that would do. What sort of relationship had she had with her father? Had she been close to him? All he knew about her family background was her parents had divorced when she was young and her father had been given custody after a protracted battle in the courts. Her mother had died of an accidental prescription drug overdose a few months later, which might or might not have been suicide.

'She has a limp.'

'Let's hope her looks make up for that. Is she hot?'

Trust his younger brother to be so shallow. Luiz was a serial model dater. If a woman hadn't been on a catwalk he wasn't interested. Alejandro thought *he* was a little picky over his partners but Luiz took it to a whole new level. No woman with a university degree need apply. Luiz didn't want intelligent conversation. He didn't stay with a woman long enough to engage her in one. He changed partners as quickly as he changed horses in a polo match. Not that *he* could talk.

'She has the sort of looks that grow on you.'

'So why would her old man set her up like this?'

'Her father is playing games from beyond the grave,' Alejandro said. 'He knew how much I wanted that land, and he also knew I did nothing to quell the rumours about him acquiring it less than honourably. In fact, I actively fuelled them. And since it's common knowledge I would never consider marriage again, this is his way of paying me back.'

'What's she like?'

Alejandro pictured that small defiant figure

with her piercing gaze and tightly set mouth. Her strength of will was admirable. Not many people stood up to him. Not many people had the courage to do so. Her intransigence fascinated him because he couldn't think of a woman of his acquaintance who wouldn't rush him off to the nearest marriage celebrant to secure the deal. Why was she so against the union? Was it him or was it marriage in general? Or was she, too, playing a game? Was she secretly delighted her father had selected *him* as her husband? Was she pretending to be aghast at the thought while privately she was congratulating herself on securing a prize catch?

'She's...interesting.'

Luiz gave a chuckle. 'That's not a word I've heard you use to describe a woman before. When do I get to meet her?'

'Soon.'

I have to convince her to marry me first.

Teddy stood at one of the library windows chewing her fingernails back to her shoulders in panic. Alejandro's low-slung sports car growled up the driveway and parked in front of the house like a black panther waiting to pounce. She watched as he got out from behind the wheel with the athletic ease of a man who was in superb physical condition.

She melted back against the velvet drape of the curtain in case he saw her spying on him. He was dressed in dark denim jeans and a white casual cotton shirt that made his olive-toned skin look all the more gloriously tanned. The sleeves were rolled back past his strong wrists, revealing dark curly hairs that continued to the backs of his hands with a sprinkling over his long fingers. He had a silver designer watch on his left wrist and he was wearing aviator sunglasses, adding to the air of command and control that was so damnably attractive. He was a man who was used to getting his own way. He got it in the boardroom. He got it in the bedroom.

Teddy had looked at the situation from every angle. She had consulted several lawyers and they had all said much the same thing. It would be a costly exercise getting her father's will overturned and even then she might not be successful. And it could take years. She couldn't afford to spend money she didn't have, or at least not *that* sort of money. If she agreed to follow the terms of the will, in six months she would be in full possession of Marlstone Manor. There would be no money worries, no sleepless nights panicking about finding the funds for the expensive upkeep of the stately mansion and grounds. She could concentrate on her art as well as provide a secure home for her loyal and loving staff.

But the thing that had decided her over all others was a phone call from her second cousin. Hugo had made his intentions clear. Marlstone Manor would be sold as soon as he took possession. He wanted the money. The house meant nothing to him. The staff meant even less.

Teddy figured a short-term marriage to Alejandro Valquez was the smaller price to pay. Being married to an attractive man who would not make any unnecessary demands on her because he said it was to be a paper marriage.

And you believed him? a voice inside her head asked.

Of course she did. Why wouldn't she? She wasn't the type of girl he would go for. His last girlfriend had been close to six foot tall with a willowy figure and waist-length blonde hair. And long legs, both in excellent working order.

Teddy pulled in a breath that caught at her throat as Alejandro's firm purposeful footsteps sounded along the corridor. She had to get her mask in place. It wouldn't do to show how unnerved she was about the arrangement she was about to enter into with him. She had to put her ice maiden face on. Assemble her features into the cool impassive face that told everyone she didn't give a damn what they thought of her gait. She straightened her spine, put her shoulders back. Gripped her walking stick with a hand that was clammy. Nerves scraped at her stomach like scrabbling mice feet as the footsteps came closer. Her heart felt as if it was beating in her oesophagus as the door was pushed open and Alejandro came striding into the room. The room seemed to shrink as he brought in the scent of the outdoors—citrus and wood and danger.

His eyes did a lazy head to toe sweep of her figure before he greeted her with a nod. 'Miss Marlstone.'

Teddy's chin came up. She couldn't help it. She didn't like the way he mocked her with that glittering look in his pitch-black gaze. She had decided against dressing shabbily. But she hadn't pulled out her best outfit, either. She'd settled for simple and casual—not much different from what he was wearing. Jeans and a cotton shirt, but she had draped a sweater across her shoulders because, in spite of the Indian summer they were experiencing, the late September weather was occasionally unpredictable. She hadn't bothered with make-up because she rarely wore it. But now, with him looking at her with that indolent gaze, she wished she had layered it on with a trowel to disguise the traitorous blush she could feel crawling over her cheeks. 'Señor Valquez.'

A corner of his mouth twitched as if he found her stiff formality amusing. 'Am I to believe you've agreed to become my wife?'

She sent him a glowering look. 'Your *paper* wife.'

'Ah, yes.' He glanced at his watch. 'You're in under the time limit. Just.'

Something inside Teddy's stomach dropped. 'You surely wouldn't expect me to agree to anything else? We're all but strangers.'

His crooked smile was knee-weakening. 'You don't normally sleep with strangers?'

'Certainly not.' She wished she hadn't sounded quite so priggish. 'I mean…I like to get to know someone first. To see if we're…erm…compatible.'

'How many lovers have you had?'

Teddy's eyes flared. 'I beg your pardon?'

His eyes held hers. Dark. Probing. Intelligent. 'Lovers. How many?'

She gave him an arch look. 'How many have *you* had?'

The glint in his eyes made her stomach slip again. 'Too many to count.'

Teddy could feel her blush burning across her cheeks like a spreading flame. Her mind was suddenly full of images of him with his beautiful bedmates, writhing and cavorting in passion, their perfect bodies in the throes of ecstasy. No hint of awkwardness or shame.

Her one and only sexual encounter had left her embarrassed and ashamed. She blamed herself for not recognising the way she had been set up. She should have known better. Men were all about the physical. They were turned on by the visual. It was how they were wired. How could she have thought Ross Jenner would be different? He had befriended her in her last year at art school and then betrayed her. He had boasted to his mates on social media about how he had done the deed with the girl no one else wanted. He had won a dare to sleep with her. He had been *paid* to do it. The memory of it still sat like a cold hard stone in her belly.

Teddy moved away from the heat of Alejandro's dark gaze to the desk where Henry had set out a drinks tray. The one thing she could do on automatic pilot was to be a polite hostess, even if it made her grind her teeth to powdered chalk. 'Would you care for a drink?'

'Whisky. No ice.'

She poured the whisky into a crystal tumbler and silently handed it to him, careful not to come into contact with his fingers. She kept her gaze out of reach of his, staring at the button of his shirt as if it was the most fascinating thing she had ever seen.

He was the most fascinating thing she had ever seen. He dominated the room like a giant in a doll's house. So tall her neck ached from keeping eye contact. So self-assured and so impossibly gorgeous her breath was having trouble moving in and out of her lungs.

He smelt delicious. The tang of his lemon and lime aftershave teased her nostrils, making her think of sun-drenched lemon groves.

And sex.

Teddy leaned on her stick as she turned to fix herself a drink. Since when did she think of sex? Hot, sweaty sex. Animal sex. Not with some weedy geek at art school who had won a bet.

Sex with a full-blooded man in his prime.

'I would like us to be married as soon as possible.'

Her left hand shook as she poured a shot of

brandy into a glass. 'We have a month before the deadline.'

'No point stalling. The sooner we marry, the sooner we end it.'

His comment shouldn't have made her feel resentful. It shouldn't have felt like an insult. She didn't want to be married to him any longer than she had to. She would have said the same to him if she'd got in first. It was damned annoying she hadn't. 'Indeed.' She gave him a gelid look. 'I couldn't have expressed it better myself.'

He moved to the windows to look at the view. 'Nice place you have here. Have you lived here long?'

'All my life.'

He turned and looked at her but because the sunlight was behind him his expression was masked by shadow. 'You do realise you'll have to come to Argentina with me.' He didn't pose it as a question but as a statement of fact.

Teddy gripped the crystal glass so tightly she thought it might explode in her hand. He wanted her to go with him? *To live with him?* She hadn't planned on going anywhere. A paper marriage was just a signed piece of paper. She didn't have to live with him. She just had to be married to him.

Didn't she?

'Surely that's not necessary?'

'You have a strange notion of what constitutes a marriage, Miss Marlstone.'

'But you said it was to be a marriage on paper.' She gripped the glass a little tighter. 'We don't have to live together. Lots of couples spend time apart, especially when they both have important careers.'

'I'm not leaving anything open to speculation.'

'But I have commitments here.'

'Cancel them.'

Teddy's back stiffened. 'Why don't you cancel yours?'

He had the audacity to chuckle at her suggestion. 'I run a multimillion dollar business. I have staff who depend on me for their wages. I need to be on site to make sure things run as smoothly as possible. Your work is transportable, isn't it?'

She gave him an intractable look. 'Yes, but I prefer to work here. I have my studio here.'

'I can give you a room at my villa. In fact, you can have a whole floor. Think of it as a working holiday, all expenses paid.'

Teddy pursed her lips in thought. It was only six months and she'd always wanted to visit Argentina. The sense of adventure appealed but living with a man she didn't know—didn't even like—was more than a little disquieting.

'Be assured I will make no demands on you.'

The words dropped into the silence, making her feel as if he had the power to read her mind. Somehow that was even more disquieting than sharing a house with him for six months.

But then the feminine part of her felt another sense of pique. Did he have to make it so obvious he found her so physically repulsive?

She knew she wasn't in-your-face beautiful. She had always been a little on the plain side. It was another thing her father had been so bitterly disappointed about in her. Not only hadn't she been born a boy, she'd had the looks to compensate for the missing Y chromosome.

'What will you tell your friends and family about our...situation?'

'My brother knows the truth and, of course, our legal team, but that's where it stops. I want everyone else to believe it's a genuine love match. It goes without saying that I would like you to refrain from speaking to the press.'

Teddy wished he'd step out of the shadows so she could see his face. Was he mocking her again? Surely he didn't think anyone would believe a man like him would fall for a girl like her? They would laugh at the suggestion. What was his motivation? Was this about his broken engagement? She had seen the press articles online about his fiancée jilting him on the day of the wedding. It would be a difficult thing for any man to face but having it splashed all over the media would have made it so much worse. Had he decided it was time to show he had moved on, so to speak? Ten years was a long time to nurse a broken heart. But had it been his heart or his pride that had taken the greatest hit?

'Are you the type of man to fall in love so quickly?'

He made a sound that was part snort, part laugh. 'I might have been once.'

Teddy pinned down her lower lip with her teeth. She couldn't help feeling sorry for the idealistic young man he must have been back then.

He stepped away from the windows and came over to the tray of drinks on the desk, pouring himself another couple of fingers of whisky. She watched as he held the glass up to his lips, watched the strong tanned column of his throat as he tossed the contents back and swallowed. He had a frown between his brows that suddenly made him seem far older than his thirty-four years. Was he thinking of his fiancée? Of the love he had lost? It would have been a terrible shock to find the woman he loved had changed her mind, only to hook up with a much older and much richer man the week after. Was he thinking of the pain the public break-up had caused him?

Teddy found it hard to imagine him falling in love with someone. He didn't seem the type. He was too hard-nosed and cynical. Too determined on having his way to give or compromise in a relationship. He was a playboy. A player, not a stayer. He changed partners as if they were disposable items. He had throwaway relationships that meant nothing to him other than a bit of temporary entertainment. She couldn't imagine him wanting to settle down and bring up a family. He didn't seem the type of man to be content with one woman. Not while he had a smorgasbord of beauties to feast on.

'What about you, Miss Marlstone?' The frown suddenly relaxed as his cynical smile returned. 'Are you the type of woman to impulsively fall in love?'

'No.'

He studied her for a long moment. 'You sound very assured.'

'That's because I am.'

'Have you ever been in love?'

'No.'

The amused glint was back in his dark eyes. 'So how do you know you won't do so quickly or impulsively?'

Teddy felt the heat of his gaze all over her body. What was it about this man that made her think of sex all the time? It was crazy. It was totally out of character. It was as if he could set her on fire with a look. She became aware of her breasts behind the sensible white cotton of her bra, aware of her inner core that flickered on and off like a faulty light switch. When she quickly moistened her dry lips a rush of sensation flowed through her as she imagined what it would feel like to have his mouth pressed to hers. To have his tongue search for hers, to play with it, tease it and provoke it into a firestorm of passion. To have his arms gather her close, to have him crush her against his strong, powerful body.

To feel.

'I'm not the impulsive type.'

His mouth tilted a little further in that fallen angel's smile that wreaked such havoc on her equilibrium. She felt dizzy from being in his presence, from being so close to him she could smell the danger he represented. It was like an exotic potion wafting in the atmosphere.

She was breathing it in—breathing *him* in.

'No?'

She suppressed a tiny shudder. 'No.'

His eyes roved over her face, lingering for a

moment on her mouth. When he reconnected his gaze with hers the frown was back between his brows. 'I should warn you about the press. They can be ferocious. I'll do my best to protect you, but there will be times when you'll just have to ignore what they say.'

Teddy wondered if he was concerned about her or himself. Why would he care what the press said about her? Once the six months was up she would be out of his life. He wouldn't have to spare her another thought. It would be his reputation he would be most concerned about. What would the press make of his choice of bride? Would comparisons be made? Of course they would and she would be found lacking in every way imaginable. 'I hope I don't cause you any unnecessary embarrassment.'

His frown deepened the trench between his eyes. 'In what way?'

She forced herself to hold his gaze without flinching. Could he see how much it pained her to be thought so undesirable? So unattractive her father had to go to such ridiculous—*insulting*—lengths to secure a husband for her? It was so demeaning to be handed over like a parcel no one wanted. It confirmed every fear she had harboured about herself since her mother had left when she was seven. She wasn't good enough, pretty enough. Lovable enough. 'I'm nothing like your last choice of bride.'

He was still looking at her with a frowning expression. 'So?'

'So they'll wonder what you see in me.'

Something passed over his features, a tiny flicker of an emotion she couldn't quite identify. 'It's not your limp that was the first thing I noticed about you. It's that chip on your shoulder.'

Teddy sent him a hardened look. 'Why wouldn't I have a chip on my shoulder? Men like you and your brother make it easy to be cynical. You only date women who look perfect. You don't even notice women like me.'

He stood looking at her for a long moment. She wished she hadn't spoken. She wished she hadn't exposed her insecurities. She wished she didn't feel so inadequate. If she had poise and sophistication she would marry him without a qualm. Most women would snatch at the chance to be linked to him for six minutes, let alone six months. He was the ultimate prize—rich and handsome and charming.

But he was someone else's prize. Not hers. Girls like her didn't get the prize. They didn't get the guy. They didn't get the fairy tale. They didn't even get the poisoned apple or the big bad wolf. They were left alone.

'There will be legal paperwork to see to before we are married,' he said as if the tense moment had not occurred. 'A celebrant will perform the ceremony in private. I don't want any press around. We will announce our marriage as a fait accompli.'

'What if I want a big white wedding with all the trimmings?' She only asked it to get under his skin and it worked.

The tic in his jaw was visible for a beat or two. 'Do you?'

Yes. Teddy thought of her mother's dress and veil wrapped in layers of blue tissue paper in the camphor chest in the attic. How many times had she climbed those stairs when no one was around and opened that chest to touch the French lace and the voluminous veil? Breathing in the faint trace of her mother's perfume that somehow, after all these years, still lingered on the fabric, like dreams that weren't yet ready to be discarded.

Teddy closed the lid on her dreams, the metaphorical slam of it feeling like a bang against her heart. 'No, but I'm just say—'

'Many couples save themselves the time and effort and expense of a wedding by eloping. The goal is to get married. Not to entertain a crowd of people you've never met or barely know and will likely never see again.'

She couldn't quite let it go. 'That's not what you thought ten years ago.'

His eyes held hers in a heated lock that made the back of her neck prickle. 'My people will speak to your people.' He gave her a brisk nod. '*Buenas tardes.*'

CHAPTER THREE

A COUPLE OF days later Alejandro frowned as he clicked on a news link on his phone. There was a photograph of Teddy and a separate one of him with the caption: *For Love or Money? Argentinian Playboy Desperate for Cash?* The short piece was damning in every way imaginable. It speculated on their relationship, hinting at a soon-to-be-conducted private wedding. It questioned his motives for the alliance. It made him look like every type of cad intent on marrying an heiress for her fortune. There was no mention of Teddy's motives. The journalist failed to mention that Alejandro had ten times the wealth of Teddy's father. His business brand would be damaged. It was one thing being seen as a party-loving playboy but quite another to be labelled a cash-strapped cad. Shareholders would pull their funds out of the company. It would destabilise everything to have investors shifting their interests right now.

How had this leaked? Had Teddy spoken to the press? Had she deliberately set out to make him look as ruthless and self-serving as she could?

He'd thought he was getting to know her. He'd thought he was coming to understand her prickliness and coolness of manner as a defence mechanism rather than who she really was on the inside. He'd thought she was different, that she was an old-fashioned girl caught up in the machinations of her unprincipled father. He'd even *liked* her, damn it.

He ground his teeth. She wanted a white wedding and was going about getting one come hell or high water. She was forcing him. Manipulating him.

Two could play at that game.

'Don't look out of the window,' Audrey said to Teddy. 'There are press everywhere. There's even one in the hedge down by the gate. I saw the glint of his camera in the sunlight.'

'What are they doing here?'

Audrey pointed to the newspaper lying on the breakfast table. 'My guess is your cousin's been making mischief. He had his hopes on getting everything if you defaulted on the will. You've upset the applecart by agreeing to the terms. He didn't think you'd do it.'

Teddy chewed the right side of her mouth as she read the article. It wasn't very flattering towards Alejandro. But it was even worse for her. It made her sound like a hideous witch the poor man had been forced to marry to keep him from the poorhouse.

Her phone beeped from inside her pocket and she took it out to see Alejandro's number come up on the screen. 'Hello?'

'I'm five minutes away,' Alejandro said. 'Pack a bag. We're going to London.'

'Why?'

'To buy a wedding dress. What else?'

'But I thought—?'

The phone snapped off.

Teddy was waiting for Alejandro in the morning room. She was standing with her back to the windows when he came in. Dressed in dark blue cotton trousers and a loose sweater and with her face free of make-up and her hair in a tight ponytail, she looked as if she was barely out of her teens. Her expression was cool and unaffected but her hand gripping her stick was white-knuckled. 'I'm not going to London with you.'

Alejandro wasn't used to people ignoring his orders. When he said 'jump' people jumped. 'I told you not to speak to the press.'

Her chin came up and her eyes glittered like diamonds in a grey lake. 'I didn't speak to the press. That was my cousin's work.'

He frowned as he took that in. It was a shock to find he had misjudged her. He wasn't used to being wrong. Apologising wasn't his strong point. Mostly because he made sure he never was wrong. 'What did you tell him about our relationship?'

'I didn't tell him anything. He figured it out for himself.' Her grey-blue eyes were brittle with resentment. 'A man like you with a woman like me? It's hardly credible, is it?'

He hadn't realised until now how unflattering

the article had been to her. She was hurt. Just like she had been the other day when she'd said she was nothing like his fiancée. He hadn't paid much attention to it at the time. Most women had petty little grievances over their appearance. Their compliment-seeking comments about feeling fat or having bad hair days annoyed him. But for Teddy it was much more serious, especially in the current culture of body beautiful. She carried her stick with such defiant pride but he could see now how much it must pain her to be unable to do the things other young women her age took for granted.

'Then perhaps we'd better make it look credible.'

Her eyes took on a wary look. 'How?'

'By being seen together.'

She dropped her gaze from his and limped over to stand behind the back of a Louis XV chair. 'Is that really necessary?'

'That's what most affianced couples do, is it not?'

She kept holding onto the back of the chair as if she was afraid she would fall without it. 'I said

I'll marry you. I did not say I would parade in public with you like a lovesick teenager.'

'Why do you let what people say upset you so much?'

'I'm not upset.'

He took in her tightly set features. 'Yes, you are. You're fuming at the injustice of it. The way everyone looks at your stick instead of at you as a person. They judge you before you get a chance to say a thing.'

She gave him an arch look. 'Like you did when you stormed in here just now?'

Alejandro accepted that with good grace. 'I was wrong. I'm sorry.'

She pressed her lips together. 'I'm not going to London with you. I don't want a wedding dress.'

'I thought all girls wanted—'

'I would prefer not to have people gawking at me as I limp up the aisle, collectedly holding their breath in case I trip or fall flat on my face.' She gave what appeared to be an involuntary shudder. 'I couldn't bear it.'

He held her look for a long beat. 'Is it because your father is no longer here to give you away?'

She gave him a speaking look. 'I think we could safely say that's one job he made sure he completed before he died, don't you?'

'I still think it's a crying shame you don't get to wear a proper wedding dress,' Audrey said as she fussed over Teddy's hair the morning of the ceremony two weeks later. 'We could've got your mother's dress tizzied up. I'm sure it's still in the attic somewhere. Remember how you used to love dressing up in it as a child?'

Teddy put a hand over her fluttering stomach. 'I wouldn't dream of exposing Mum's dress to a marriage that isn't real. It would be sacrilege.'

'Speaking of sacrilege...' Audrey tut-tutted as she pinned a tendril of Teddy's hair in place '...not being married in a church? It's positively heathen, if you ask me. And no witnesses, apart from strangers? What's the world coming to?'

'It's what Alejandro wants.' And what Alejandro wanted he got.

It was hard to believe this was her wedding day. It felt surreal. As if she were in a dream that wasn't turning out the way she had expected.

There was no romance. No sense of excitement and joy at having found a soulmate. There was no sense of anticipation for the future, of having children and bringing them up in a home filled with love and harmony.

It was cold and formal like a business deal. The legal formalities had been seen to; the documents were signed. The next six months she would be living in Argentina with Alejandro as his wife.

On paper.

Those two words were supposed to be reassuring but somehow they niggled at her like a pebble in her shoe. It was inconsistent of her to be feeling so out of sorts. It wasn't as if she was interested in him physically. Well, that wasn't *quite* the truth. He was potently attractive and every moment she spent with him she had to do her level best to ignore the impact he had on her senses.

He had a way of looking at her with those black-as-midnight eyes, as if he were seeing through the layers of her clothes, heating up every inch of her flesh. Making her aware of her body in a way she hadn't been before. Making her aware of needs and wants she had denied for most of her adult life.

Would he continue to look at her like that once she was living with him? Or would he ignore her while he got on with his playboy life, leaving her to spend her days like a wife from the old days when rich men had numerous mistresses on the go and no one blinked an eye?

Would he be discreet or blatant about his affairs? Why did she even care? What did it have to do with her? It wasn't as if she even liked him. How could she like someone who had come charging into her life and taken control in such an overbearing manner?

Audrey stood back to look at her with a sigh. 'You look beautiful. Your mother would be very proud of you.'

Teddy looked at her reflection in the cheval mirror. She knew she wasn't going to cut it for the cover of *Vogue* or anything, but at least she looked presentable. The classic Chanel-style suit in a shell-pink suited her colouring. So too did the pearls around her throat and the studs in her ears.

Her hair was in a smooth knot at the back of her head and her make-up understated and yet somehow managing to make the most of her deep-set eyes, bringing out the grey and the blue in a way that was almost startling—even if she said so herself.

Her lips were painted with a shimmery lipgloss and her high cheekbones defined by bronzer, making her look sophisticated, regal and poised. She usually stayed away from dresses but the silk stockings Audrey had talked her into buying were as fine as gossamer and made her feel feminine.

Her eyes went to the tissue-wrapped mid-height heels in the box on the floor. 'Do you think I should risk it?'

Audrey picked up the box and handed her a shoe. 'You should.'

Teddy slipped her feet into the heels, holding onto Audrey's arm for support. 'I won't be able to wear them for long. And what if I make a fool of myself and fall over?'

'Alejandro will be there to catch you. That's what husbands are for.'

'He isn't going to be that sort of husband.' She smoothed the dress over her hips, testing her balance, all the while trying to ignore the funny little pang that was burrowing its way below her heart like a corkscrew. 'Six months and this will be over the way it began. With a couple of signatures on a piece of paper.'

'At least you'll both have what you want.' Audrey, ever pragmatic, gave Teddy a reassuring smile. 'He'll have his land and you'll have your home.'

But what if I want more?

Teddy pushed the thought aside as she reached for the posy of flowers Stan had picked first thing that morning. She breathed in the heady scent of David Austin Autumn Damask roses, wondering if she would ever smell a rose in future without thinking of the day she had married a man for what he could give her instead of how much he loved her.

Alejandro checked his watch. Beads of sweat were working their way down between his shoulder blades. He *hated* weddings. Yes, even private civil ones without a single camera in sight. They made his gut churn. They made his head pound. They made him want to punch something.

It brought back the humiliation of ten years ago. The shock of finding he'd been jilted. He could still feel the cold dread that moved through him as he'd looked down the aisle of the cathedral. The long *empty* aisle with the sea of faces either side looking at him at first in expectation, then in embarrassment and then in pity.

His scalp crawled at the memory.

His insides twisted and festered with bitterness.

He had stood there for over an hour, stupidly hoping it was a traffic jam, a hiccup with one of the bridesmaids or a wardrobe malfunction— anything but the truth. How could he not have known? How could he have been so gullible to believe Mercedes Delgado had loved him? She had loved his money, or she had until someone came along who had more. A man old enough to be her father. A sugar daddy. A meal ticket. The man most women secretly wanted even though they flatly denied it.

A decade on and Alejandro still couldn't bear the smell of roses. The church had been full of them, picked from the rose garden his father had planted for his mother when they were first married. Every time he walked past that garden the cloying scent of betrayal was enough to make him want to puke. The day his father died he had bulldozed the roses into the ground.

He glanced at the door. What was taking Teddy so long? It was a private ceremony, for God's sake. If they didn't get a move on the press might turn up. After the phone-tapping scandal a couple of years ago, no one felt safe. He had managed to keep things quiet over the last couple of weeks, keeping his contact with her to an absolute minimum. The occasional phone call to sort out business, the odd text or email to check a detail or to let her know the travel arrangements, but no more visits to her home. He hadn't wanted the press to tail him, nor had he wanted to give her any more opportunities to get under his skin. She had an annoying habit of being able to needle him when he least expected it.

He still hadn't made up his mind about her.

Was she quiet and shy and uncertain of herself or was she calculating and devious? As devious and calculating as her father? Had her old man cooked up this scheme with her? Clark Marlstone had known how much Alejandro hated him for how he had swindled his father. Was this his way of keeping the upper hand beyond the grave?

A marriage of convenience was still a marriage. It was still anathema to him and anyone who did an internet search on him would know why.

Alejandro checked his watch at the same time the celebrant sent him a questioning look. 'Don't worry. She'll be here.'

She'd better be or I'll not be answerable for the consequences.

'Am I late?' Teddy glanced at Audrey's watch. 'Oh, God, I'm going to be late.'

'It's fashionable for the bride to be late.'

'I'm not fashionable and I'm not a bride.'

'Pretend.'

Teddy drew in a breath to calm her buzzing nerves. 'Right. Pretend. I can do that.'

This was so different from how she'd imagined a wedding day should be. It was cold and sterile. A heartless union on paper. It didn't mean anything. It was a formality that had no emotional investment. The ache inside her chest widened; it foamed and frothed and rose up, threatening to suffocate her. This was a travesty. A farce. A mockery of all she held sacred. Thank God Alejandro hadn't asked for a church ceremony. That would have been asking too much of her. To stand in front of an altar and lie would be against every principle she possessed. How could she promise to love someone she didn't even like?

You do like him.

'No, I don't.'

Audrey frowned. 'Did you say something?'

Teddy swallowed a tight knot of panic. 'I wonder if he's thought to buy a ring. Do you think he has? I didn't tell him my size. Would he have guessed? I'd hate to have one that was too tight or too loose. Do you think he—?'

Audrey covered her hand with her work-worn

papery thin one and gave it a tiny squeeze. 'You don't have to go through this if you don't want to. It's not too late to back out. You do know that, don't you?'

Teddy bit her lip. 'I can't do that to him. It would be too cruel for words.'

Audrey smiled a knowing smile as she patted Teddy's hand. 'That's what I thought.'

Teddy walked into the register office on legs that felt as unsteady as a newborn foal's but it had nothing to do with her limp or the fact she was wearing heels. Nerves were getting the better of her. She tried to be composed and calm but the enormity of what she was doing was eating at her stomach lining like battery acid.

She was getting married. To a man she barely knew. She was flying with him in his private jet to his home in Argentina as soon as the officialdom was over. Her bags had been sent to his hotel. She had said her tearful goodbyes to her staff, promising them she would be back in six months to take over the running of the estate as she had always planned to do as her father's only child and heir. It was her birthright. So what if she had to give up six months of her life to claim it? It would be worth it. She would be financially secure for the rest of her life.

This wasn't a real wedding. She wasn't a real bride. This was a process she had to go through to inherit what was rightfully hers. It was a paper marriage. It was a means to an end. A hands-off affair that would be over before she knew it.

She was being silly for having jitters.

Only *real* brides had those.

Alejandro was standing stiffly in front of the celebrant, who was dressed in an off-the-peg suit. She knew that because it was so obvious next to Alejandro's bespoke tailoring. He looked so handsome and so debonair and so far out of her league it was laughable. She didn't know whether to be relieved or disappointed there were no cameras around to document the event. Without photographic evidence, who on earth would believe Alejandro had married *her*?

But of course he wouldn't want cameras around. He wouldn't want a repeat of ten years ago. He would not announce their marriage until it was signed and sealed.

The press's interest had fizzled out a few days after Hugo's mischief-making but it would soon be reactivated once the official announcement was made. The same horrible comments and comparisons would be made. She would be laughed at, felt sorry for. Pitied for being married to a man who hadn't chosen her for love but for money. If he had been worried about his reputation being sullied by the aspersions her cousin had cast he'd shown no sign of it since. It was business as usual.

'Sorry I'm late. It took longer than I expected to get ready.'

His dark eyes narrowed as they went to the posy of roses in her hand. A dull flush rose along his cheekbones and the line of his mouth looked taut. Grim. Chalk-white at the edges. 'Let's get on with it.'

Teddy suppressed a frown for the sake of the celebrant but then she wondered if Alejandro had given the man the heads-up. It seemed unlikely, given he wanted to keep the truth about their relationship under wraps.

She stood beside him as the brief ceremony began. Alejandro was standing so rigidly she could feel his tension emanating from him even though he barely moved. Even his breathing was minimal, as if he had every faculty of his body under the severest control.

She wondered if he was thinking of his other wedding day—the day when his fiancée failed to turn up. Over four hundred guests witnessed his humiliation. How much of that disappointment made him the man he was today? Was his driven workaholic focus a hoofprint of the bitterness he felt from being jilted?

Teddy knew all about rejection. She had spent most of her life feeling inadequate. Her father had never bothered to hide the fact he had longed for a son. Her arrival had been the death knell to his marriage to her mother. He had only fought for custody, dragging it through the courts for as long as he could, because he wanted to win the battle against her mother, not because he wanted *her*.

Weren't his beyond the grave machinations proof of that?

Her father had been prepared to let her degenerate second cousin inherit his entire estate if she didn't toe the line. It was his way of controlling her. Having a say in her life. He hadn't trusted she would be capable of managing her own life. He had always intervened, criticised, blamed.

He had even blamed her for the accident when she was ten years old when really it was his fault for insisting she ride a horse that was far too headstrong and flighty for her. Instead of being grateful she hadn't been killed when it threw her, her father had made it blatantly obvious he was disappointed in her recovery. Why hadn't she got rid of the limp? It was only a broken hip. It should have healed by now. Hadn't she done the right exercises during rehab? Why couldn't she try harder? No one wanted a girl with an ungainly limp. How would she be able to have a child one day if she couldn't walk properly? Who would want her?

No one.

Which was why she was participating in this cold, heartless ceremony, where there was nothing romantic about the words spoken. The impersonal exchange of vows was as far from her girlish dreams as anything could be. The simple white gold wedding ring was a perfect fit as Alejandro slipped it on her finger. But it was hard not to feel tainted by the process. It made her feel like she had cheated on a test. She was a fraud. A liar. A fake.

'You may kiss the bride.'

The words jolted her. Shocked her. *Excited her.*

But Alejandro's response was like a slap in the face. 'That won't be necessary.'

Teddy fixed a smile in place. 'We're not the touchy-feely type,' she said to the celebrant. 'I mean not in public. In private, well, that's another thing.' She gave her eyes an expressive little fluttery roll. 'You would *not* believe what we get up to. It would be enough to make your hair curl. Oh…your hair is already curly.'

The celebrant gave them both a forced smile

that barely moved the edges of his thin lips. 'I have another ceremony to conduct. Excuse me.'

Alejandro took her by the elbow, his fingers sinking into her flesh like a bite. 'We need to have some ground rules.'

Teddy had trouble keeping up with his frog-marching pace. 'Do you mind not rushing me? I don't want to trip over. I'm not used to wearing heels.'

He slowed his pace and his hold loosened a fraction. 'I'm sorry.' He said it grudgingly as if apologising was unfamiliar to him.

She shrugged off his hand and pointedly rubbed at her elbow. 'Speaking of ground rules, I don't want you to touch me.'

'I will have to touch you in public. It will appear odd if I don't.'

'You weren't too keen on touching me in front of the celebrant.' Teddy knew she sounded churlish. She hadn't wanted him to kiss her. *Had she?*

His expression was difficult to read. 'Were you disappointed?'

'Of course not.'

His gaze went to the posy in her hand as a muscle worked in his jaw. 'Why the roses?'

'They're my favourite flower. Stan, the gardener, picked them for me first thing this morning.'

'Get rid of them.'

Teddy frowned. 'What?'

'You heard.'

She gripped the posy a little tighter. 'You can't tell me what to do—hey, what are you doing?'

He ripped the posy out of her grasp and tossed it in the nearest rubbish bin before turning back to glare at her. 'Ground rule number one. No roses.'

Teddy refused to be intimidated by him, even though she had never seen him look so angry. She hadn't seen anyone look so angry. Not even her father in one of his towering rages about her mother had looked as fired up as he did right now. 'Fine. No roses. Anything else?'

His gaze tussled with hers for endless seconds. But then he let out a long breath as he scraped a hand through his hair. 'Once we're on the flight I'll make a brief announcement to the press. Let me handle the questions when we land in Buenos Aires. We have a short stopover there before we fly on to Mendoza Province. That leg of the journey is less—a little under two hours. The first leg is a little over fourteen.'

Teddy got in the chauffeur-driven car he had waiting by the kerbside. He got in beside her and immediately took out his phone and started scrolling through his messages and emails. She was being dismissed. Ignored. On her wedding day. Possibly the *only* wedding day she would ever have.

Didn't he realise how on edge she felt? This was a big event in her life. It wasn't every day a girl married a man she had only met a handful of times and travelled to a foreign country with him. He might date women who wouldn't blink an eye at such an event but she was not one of them. She hardly ever travelled. What was the point of travelling when you couldn't walk around like everyone else when you got there? Her hip didn't cope with long periods of standing and she absolutely *refused* to be pushed around in a wheelchair. So what if she was a homebody? How was that hurting anyone? At least she had a small carbon footprint, unlike someone else she could name who flew about the globe on a private jet, for pity's sake.

Teddy watched Alejandro's fingers tapping away on his phone. 'Do you ever take a break from work?'

He turned to look at her with a frown that made three vertical lines appear between his brows. 'Running a business such as mine requires focus and dedication. I'm negotiating with an architect on a resort I'm planning to build. It all takes time.'

She looked at his mouth as he spoke. The area surrounding it was dark with shadow even though he would have shaved first thing that morning. The tiny pinpricks stood out around his mouth and over his strongly defined philtrum between his nose and his top lip. His lower lip was fuller than his top lip, a fullness that hinted at the potent sensuality he possessed.

Teddy felt a dart of desire spear through her. And another. And another. Hot little spurts of longing that arrowed out from the centre of her womanhood. She wondered what his mouth would feel like pressing down on hers, sweeping her up into a vortex of thrilling sensations. She pressed her knees together but the sensation was still there. Hunger. Need. Pulsing want.

She could smell the lime notes of his aftershave cologne. It was sharp and fresh and it made her want to lean closer to breathe in more of his scent. She was aware of his long muscled thighs on the seat beside her. His broad shoulders were only inches from hers. They were breathing in the same air. It made her feel as if an intimate boundary had been subtly crossed.

Her gaze went to his. Locked on his. He looked tired about the eyes, the fine skin beneath them grey and drawn as if he hadn't been sleeping properly. 'Maybe I could help you while I'm—'

'That won't be necessary.' The words were clipped and stung her much more than they should have. He turned back to his phone and started tapping in an email.

That won't be necessary. Was that his stock phrase? Loosely translating to: *You're* not necessary. Was this how it was going to be? He would only speak to her when he wanted to? Only interact with her when it suited him?

Just like her father had done.

He'd used her to fill in the odd dull moment but had no real desire for her company.

She had been a trophy daughter and now she was a trophy bride.

'There's no need to be rude. I was only offering to—'

'Miss Marlstone—' he acknowledged her quirked eyebrow at his formal address with a little flicker of his eyelids and continued '—Teddy. Let me make myself clear from the outset. I do not need or require your help.'

'But surely—'

'Do you *ever* do what you're told?' There were white tips at the corners of his mouth and his eyes flashed in irritation.

'Fine. I won't speak unless I'm spoken to.' She mimicked a zipping motion over her mouth. 'See? No more speaking.'

He held her gaze for a long beat. Then his eyes slipped downwards to look at her mouth.

Paused there. Burned there so hotly she could feel it through every layer of her skin.

Time ground to a halt. Her breathing came to a standstill. Her heart thudded. Skipped a beat and then sprinted as his hand came to her chin, holding it between two of his fingers as his eyes meshed with hers.

Teddy swallowed thickly. Pushed the tip of her tongue out to sweep over the last of her lipgloss. 'You said a paper marriage.' She was surprised her voice came out at all, let alone so evenly.

His eyes were still hooded and trained on her mouth. 'That was the plan.'

Was? Her heart jolted against her ribcage. What did he mean, 'was'? Was he thinking about shifting the goalposts on their arrangement? Changing the rules? *Breaking the rules?* A trickle of traitorous excitement flowed through her at the thought of him making love to her, of his long strong body possessing hers. Enrapturing hers in a feast of the senses that so far she had only ever imagined.

But then she thought of his motivations. He wouldn't want her because he was attracted to her. He would only want her because she was conveniently available. Men could do that. They could separate the act of sex from feelings. All cats were black in the dark, as the crude saying went.

Another beat of silence.

'You should let go of my chin.' *And stop making me want to kiss you so badly I can't think about anything but how sexy and male and tempting your mouth is.*

His thumb brushed over the base of her chin. 'What if I don't?'

Teddy disguised a gulp. 'You'd be breaking the rules.'

A corner of his mouth came up in a sexy slant of a smile. 'What if I wanted to break the rules?'

She couldn't stop staring at his mouth. Couldn't stop lusting after his mouth. It was so impossibly sexy when he smiled like that. It made her knees turn to liquid and her belly quiver uncontrollably. Her lips tingled as if he had already pressed his mouth to hers. She could feel the restless energy under the surface of her skin as if the sensitive nerves were assembling, waiting, anticipating the first fiery brush of his mouth on hers. 'Y…you don't want to do that.'

'Why not?' He brought his mouth close to hers, letting his warm hint of mint breath skate over her lips, teasing her, tantalising her with the promise of touchdown. 'You might like it.' He nudged her softly against the side of her nose. 'Breaking the rules can be fun.'

She shivered as his stubbly skin grazed the smooth skin of her cheek, triggering a rush of longing so intense it roared through her like a runaway flame. She felt it pulsing inside her body, a contraction, a tugging, a deep pulling sensation that made her ache with a sense of hollowness. 'I never break the rules.'

His mouth travelled to her jawline, his lips passing over her skin in a barely touching movement. Touching, then not touching. Light and soft, like the wings of a moth which couldn't make up its mind whether or not to land. She reminded herself to breathe. Concentrated on resisting the urge to search for his mouth with hers. She didn't want to be the weak one. The needy one. She didn't want him to think her so desperate for a kiss she would compromise their agreement.

She could be strong.

She *would* be strong.

Alejandro slowly eased back to look at her, his eyes dark and glittering. Knowing. 'Ground rule number two. No other men. Under any circumstances.'

Teddy gave a mental laugh. Other men? What a joke. She had forgotten what a man felt like, it had been so long since she'd been near one. Although she definitely hadn't been near any man as heart-stoppingly gorgeous as him. 'Got that. But same goes.'

His brow lifted in an arc over one of his satirical coal-black eyes. 'Here's the thing. I'm the one who makes the rules. Not you.'

She kept her gaze locked on his. 'I'm not going to be made a fool of by you sleeping around. If you want to have affairs then you'll have to afford me the same right. That's only fair.'

His smile was mocking but she sensed something angry about it too. It was in his gaze, a brittleness that warned her of the limits of how far she could push him. 'Well, well, well,' he drawled. 'The little mouse has roared.'

Teddy felt her cheeks colour up. No doubt he was resting easy, thinking no man would ever come knocking on her bedroom door. He saw her as a dried up spinster. A wallflower with no life beyond her sketchpad and paintbrushes. But she had the same urgings and yearnings as her peers.

She longed for connection, for intimacy.

For love.

Alejandro might mock her for her quiet nature and mild ways but she had fire in her spirit when she needed it. She would not allow him to dictate the terms of their relationship as if she were nothing more than a chess piece on a board.

He was only showing an interest in her now because he was bored. They had a long journey ahead and he was obviously looking for some in-flight entertainment.

She would not play unless it was for keeps.

'If you're going to continue to be a playboy during our…arrangement, then please have the decency to be discreet about it.'

'And will you be discreet, *querida?*'

Teddy's stomach folded over at the Spanish endearment. His voice stroked the word, gave it a musical, lyrical sound that reverberated in her soul. Was that how he was going to disarm her defences? Melt her self-control with almost-kisses and casually uttered endearments that fed the hunger for romance that burned deep inside her?

If so, she was dangerously, terrifyingly out-matched.

He had weapons at his disposal that would make her self-discipline collapse like a house of cards in front of a sneeze. She would have no hope of resisting him if he decided to 'break the rules'.

She looked into his ebony eyes—those eyes that saw more than she wanted him to see. Knew more than she wanted him to know. Made her feel more than she wanted to feel.

She didn't want to cross the line with him.

She had a goal. A plan.

It didn't include getting her heart broken.

But, oh, he was so darned tempting with his

teasing looks and his sensual mouth. He was everything she loathed in a man and yet was inexorably drawn to. He was worldly and casual about things she took seriously. He used people to get where he wanted to go. He was ruthless in his business dealings. He was a mover and a shaker, a taker, not a giver.

And for the next six months he was her husband.

Gulp.

CHAPTER FOUR

ALEJANDRO WORKED SOLIDLY on the flight home. He used it as a distraction from watching the sleeping figure of Teddy lying in the capsule seat/bed beside him. He was conscious of her in a way he didn't want to be. Aware of her far more than he'd expected. Her quiet intensity enthralled him. Fascinated him. She looked so demure and malleable and yet she had a will of steel. She reminded him of a velvet-covered brick.

He smiled when he thought of her trying to lay down the rules. If she wanted to mess around then she could mess around with him. He wasn't as profligate as his younger brother but he enjoyed sex for the mindless release it gave him. There was nothing like a bit of monkey sex to get his mind off his responsibilities. He liked her spirit. It was the biggest turn on. There was something about her that connected with him in a way no one had done before. She was book-ish but not boring. She had a classic understated beauty and her limp gave her an air of vulner-ability that spoke to the protective side of his nature.

He had come close to kissing her in the car. The temptation of her mouth had drawn him in like a lure. The silk of her skin as he touched her made his blood thicken in his veins. Her mouth was soft and full—a sensual fullness that spoke of a passionate nature beneath that starchy veneer she put on. Her hair was a rich dark brown, with glossy highlights that caught the light now and again. Her nose was small and neat and uptilted. An aristocrat's nose. Proud. Haughty. But that was what he liked about her. She had dignity.

He was reluctant to admit it but he was getting a little tired of the sycophants that surrounded him. No one ever said no to him. No one ever crossed him. No one ever defied him. He could have any woman he wanted with just a look or a smile.

His sexual encounters were connections of bodies, not minds. But lately he had been feeling a little short-changed. Another hotel room. Another encounter. An exchange of phone numbers, even though he knew he wasn't going to call.

He hadn't spent the whole night with anyone since his fiancée. Allowing someone that close was unthinkable. He didn't have time for post-coital snuggle-ups. Once the deed was done he was ready to leave. Sharing a bed was letting someone in to areas of his life he wanted cordoned off. No one got that close to him, even though many wanted to.

Teddy Marlstone was a challenge because she didn't kowtow to him. She didn't like him and she had made it clear from the start. She was only with him because of her inheritance. She wouldn't have a bar of him otherwise. The look in her grey-blue eyes when he'd threatened to make their marriage real had amused and annoyed him in turn.

How soon would it be before he got her to change her mind?

* * *

Teddy slept for most of the flight out of sheer exhaustion from the day's events, only waking just as they came in to land. Alejandro packed up his laptop as she freshened up in preparation for landing. It appeared he had worked the whole flight as his blanket and pillow and eye cover mask were still wrapped in their protective plastic. Did the man *never* take a break from work? Was he a man or a machine? Didn't he need even a couple of hours' sleep?

He was so focused and disciplined it was unnerving. She hadn't met anyone quite so determined. Once he had a goal in sight he aimed for it like a strike missile did a target. Her father's machinations had given him a purpose. A plan. Nothing was going to stop him reclaiming his land. She had been swept up in the whirlwind of his gritty determination and would no doubt be spat out six months later when she had served her purpose.

She would have to guard against getting involved with him on any level. Not even as friends; especially not as lovers. A shiver scudded over her flesh at the thought of him touching her. Kissing her. Those sculptured lips moving over hers, his tongue delving between her lips and mating with hers. His body holding her close so she could feel the surge and swell of his proud male flesh. His blood-thickened flesh parting her thighs…

Teddy squeezed her thighs together to stop the dragging sensation in her core. She had to stop thinking about him in that way. He wasn't interested in her. Not like that. He was toying with her. He'd been doing it from the start. Mocking her for her old-fashioned values. Laughing at her with those black-as-night eyes. Curling his lip at her unsophisticated sense of dress. She was a novelty to him. A quaint diversion from his usual fare of beautiful, designer-dressed blondes. He would use her if it suited him and drop her when it didn't. It was what men like him did. He didn't need to commit. He didn't see the point in anything beyond the here and now. He lived in the moment and took what he wanted when and where and from whom he wanted it.

Teddy knew he had only insisted she come

with him to Argentina so he could continue his life without interruption. Her role as the quiet biddable wife at home would suit him down to the ground. What right would she have to complain when she was ultimately getting everything she wanted from this short alliance? Her inheritance would be secure. Her future would be settled. She would never have to worry about money once the six months was up. He was doing her a massive favour, or so he thought. He had given up his freedom so they could both achieve their goals, but so far she had been the only one to sacrifice anything. She was thousands of miles from the people she loved and the home she adored.

His life would continue as normal. He would make sure of that. It would be business as usual. Didn't he have any idea of what this was like for her? Did he have *that* much of an ego that he thought this was some sort of trip of a lifetime? She was tired and her hip was throbbing. Her head was tight from the beginnings of a tension headache. Panic fluttered in her stomach like moths with flick knives for wings.

Breathe. Breathe. Breathe.

The airport at Buenos Aires was a large modern building with a high arching roof overhead. Crowds of people were bustling everywhere as they gathered for flights or arrivals or connections.

Teddy steeled herself for the onslaught of press cameras. She hated being photographed. *Hated it.* The flash always took her by surprise. She either blinked at the wrong moment or her smile was too forced. She couldn't remember the last time anyone had taken a decent photo of her. Even her baby photos weren't anything to boast about. Too long and scrawny to be described as bonny, she had looked more like a skinned rabbit than a chubby-cheeked cherub, a fact her father had never failed to remind her of throughout her childhood.

Her teenage years had been particularly excruciating. Her father had never missed an opportunity to remind her of her limitations in the looks department. In the end she had given up trying to please him. She had deliberately dressed down, choosing outfits that were as unflattering as they were unfashionable. She dressed to be unnoticed, which was why Alejandro had looked right through her when she'd met him as a socially awkward sixteen-year-old. Up until that point she hadn't cared if she wasn't pretty enough. It hadn't bothered her at all. But when she'd seen Alejandro that day she had suddenly realised how invisible she was. She hadn't even registered on his visual radar. She was nothing. A blank space. A nobody.

Alejandro put his arm around her waist as he led her out to the arrivals area, where a press gang had gathered in anticipation of their arrival. 'Smile for the cameras, *querida*. It's show time.'

The conversation Alejandro had with the press was in Spanish so Teddy only picked up the occasional word. Photos were taken and she smiled in all the right places, but privately wondered if anyone was going to believe Alejandro's choice of bride wasn't some sort of practical joke. Never had she felt more inadequate. More hopelessly ill-prepared. More out of her depth. She was floundering in a sea of insecurity, each white-capped wave of self-doubt threatening to swamp her. She was travel-weary and dishevelled. Her hip was aching from the long journey, which made her limp all the more obvious. People were already staring at her with that pitying look. What had she been thinking to agree to this? Had she lost her senses? She didn't belong here. She didn't belong to him. She was a fraud. An impostor.

But, as if Alejandro sensed her quiet despair, he brought her even closer to his body so she could lean into his strength. 'Come, *mi amor.*' He led her towards the departure point of their connecting flight. 'We will soon be home.'

Home was a magnificent property forty minutes' drive out of Mendoza Province. The grey-green of olive groves and row after row of vines covered the fields around the villa. There seemed to be acres and acres of fertile land stretching in all directions as far as the eye could see. Glossy-coated horses grazed in verdant fields and, further on, the high planes were vegetated with lush forest, and beyond that the majestic vista of the white snow-capped Andes Mountains rose up in the distance. Cauliflower-shaped clouds were suspended in a sky of cerulean blue and the air was warm from a light breeze that had the sweet earthy smell of freshly cut grass on it.

There were various outbuildings and stables and servants' accommodation far enough away from the villa to give it a sense of seclusion and privacy.

The villa itself was a grand affair, built in a neo-classical style, four storeys high with a manmade long rectangular lake set in front. The creamy stone of the villa offset by the silver-blue of the lake was nothing short of spectacular. The stunning architecture with its palatial lines was indicative of a rich man's castle where centuries of wealth had multiplied.

Alejandro and Luiz Valquez were the next generation. But to whom would they pass their wealth when it was time for them to leave this world? They were both ardent playboys with no thought of settling down. Luiz was a notorious flirt. A charming playboy who had a reputation as a party animal. A daredevil thrill-seeker who rarely spent two nights in the one country. The thought of him settling down to marriage and babies was as likely as pigs circling overhead. Not going to happen.

Now Alejandro was stuck in a paper marriage for six months. Did it worry him that he wasn't producing an heir for this veritable fortune? Did he want to, some time in the future? Didn't all rich men want to leave a legacy to their off-spring? Wasn't it part of their DNA to want to continue their genetic line?

Alejandro took Teddy's elbow as he led her up the steps to the villa. 'Remember my staff thinks this is a real marriage. It's important to act as natural as possible whenever we're not alone.'

She gave him a sideways glance. 'I'm not one for public displays of affection. Just so you know.'

His look was largely unreadable but she thought she saw a tiny gleam in his eyes. 'I'll keep that in mind.'

A young boy of about fourteen or fifteen opened the front door of the villa. He bowed formally and welcomed them both in near perfect English but his grin was cheeky rather than deferential. 'Welcome, Señor and Señora Valquez. Congratulations on your marriage. I am very happy for you both. I am very surprised because I thought Señor Valquez was seeing a—'

'Jorge—' Alejandro's tone was curt '—Señora Valquez is tired from our journey. Go and tell Estefania and Sofi we are here.'

'But I'm only say—'

'Have you done your homework?' Alejandro asked.

The boy scowled and scuffed one of his boot-clad toes against the marble floor. 'I would rather be out with the horses.'

'I know, but in order to have a career with them you need to know much more than how to strap on a saddle and a bridle.'

Jorge slouched his shoulders. *'Si, señor.'*

Alejandro dropped his hand from Teddy's elbow once the boy had disappeared through another doorway. 'I'm sorry about his behaviour. There are a few rough edges to smooth over. He's young and a bit headstrong at times.'

Teddy looked up at him. 'Does he work for you? He seems rather young.'

'I brought him in off the streets. He's had barely any education but I'm determined to get him reading and writing at an age appropriate level, in spite of his resistance.'

She tried not to gape at him. She had no idea he was the sort of man to take in a homeless young person. It made her wonder who exactly was this enigmatic man she had married. 'He was homeless?'

'Yes. His mother remarried and his stepfather didn't take to him. His own father had been killed when he was a toddler.'

'That was kind of you…to take him in like that.'

He gave an indifferent shrug. 'I'm not running a charity but occasionally I get a good day's work out of him. I'm not holding my breath he'll amount to much.'

'All the same, he must be very grateful to you.'

'I'll get one of the staff to take your bags up.'

The subject change was as abrupt as his tone with the boy earlier. Teddy suspected he cared much more about the boy than he was letting on. Jorge couldn't be more than fifteen or so.

Had Alejandro taught him to speak English or facilitated someone else to do so? It showed a side to his character she had not been expecting. It certainly wasn't a side the press knew anything about. Taking in homeless children and schooling them and providing for them was not something hardened playboys were known for, surely?

Teddy let out a sigh of wonder as her gaze took in the mansion's grandeur. A sweeping staircase led the eye to the gallery above and the floor above that. The high vaulted ceiling with its huge crystal chandelier that hung like a frozen cascade of brilliant diamonds all but took her breath away. Priceless artwork adorned the walls; classical bronze sculptures, beautiful marble statues and busts on stands were positioned strategically to make the most of the angle of light coming in from the windows.

It was like stepping into a beautifully preserved museum. She was surrounded by hundreds of years of colourful history. All of Alejandro's ancestors looked down at her with their watchful eyes. She was suddenly conscious of being the first Valquez bride since Alejandro's father had brought home Alejandro's mother, Eloise Beauchamp, a young and beautiful Frenchwoman he had met while at a polo-playing event in France.

Were Alejandro's ancestors quietly assessing Teddy for all her shortcomings? Comparing her to the last bride who had been carried over the threshold?

Except Teddy hadn't been carried over the threshold. She hadn't even been kissed at the ceremony.

'What do you think of the villa?' Alejandro asked.

She turned in a circle to meet his gaze again. 'Somehow, I thought it would be much bigger.'

He frowned and then threw his head back and laughed. It was a deep rich sound that made the skin on her arms tingle. She had only seen him smile that cynical or mocking smile. His laugh hinted at a man who was not as forbidding as he appeared. Was he a man who could relax and have fun when the time was right?

'In keeping with my ego?'

Teddy couldn't hold back a sheepish smile. 'It's

a lovely house. Has it been in your family for a long time?'

'My ancestors came here in the colonial period at the beginning of the sixteenth century.' He pointed to a painting on the gallery above. 'That is the first of my forefathers—Juan Fernando Valquez. He built the first villa here but it was unfortunately destroyed by fire in the early eighteen-eighties. It was rebuilt some years later and our family has lived and farmed here ever since.'

She studied the dark swarthy features with the glittering eyes and strong nose and sensual mouth. 'You look like him.'

'A little, perhaps.' He gave her a glinting look. 'I'm told I'm far more ruthless.'

'That, I can believe.'

The rest of the household staff moved forward to be introduced. There was a housekeeper called Estefania and a much younger maid called Sofi. Like Jorge, Sofi was still in her teens. Teddy wondered if she was another one of Alejandro's street kids. There were several men of varying ages who worked on the estate but Alejandro told her she would meet them when they did a tour later.

If Estefania or Sofi were surprised by their employer coming home with a new wife they were either too worried about losing their jobs to remark on it or too polite to do so. Both of them smiled at her and in reasonably good English welcomed her to Casa de Valquez.

Alejandro gave instructions to the younger girl in Spanish before turning to Teddy. 'Sofi will show you to your room. I have some urgent things to see to in my office. You can settle in and rest until dinner.'

Teddy wondered if he was going to kiss her for show but he merely smiled and walked away. The sharp sting of disappointment shocked her. Even though she'd told him she wasn't keen on public displays of affection, surely a little brush on the lips wouldn't have killed him, would it?

Sofi took Teddy to a suite rather than a room. It was decorated in an Italianate style with plush watermarked satin curtains at the windows with festooned pelmets and big bow-like sashes. There was an Aubusson rug on the floor and the bed was a four-poster made from a beautifully polished mahogany. A dressing table and mirror and velvet-covered stool were against one wall and an antique wardrobe with decorative carvings and brass inlays was against the other. There was a walnut lady's writing desk and chair and a wing chair and footstool next to one of the windows, providing a lovely reading nook with views over the estate and to the stunning peaks of the mountains beyond.

The en suite bathroom was fitted out in marble, glass and brass and had a deep free-standing bath and a double shower recess with a rain shower fitting. Soft thick white towels were folded on the brass towel rack and shell-shaped cakes of soap and a variety of luxurious lotions and potions were arranged on the marble vanity in front of the gilt-framed mirror.

'Señor Valquez's room through this door, *sí*?' Sofi pointed to a door on the connecting wall.

Teddy's gaze went to the brass key in the lock. She wondered what the young girl was thinking about a newly married couple having separate rooms. Would Sofi assume Alejandro would walk through that door whenever the fancy took him? Her insides gave a little flutter at the thought.

'He is very handsome, *si*?' Sofi said.

Teddy could feel her cheeks heating. Was the girl wondering how such a handsome man would marry someone as plain as her? 'Yes. He is.'

Sofi gave a heartfelt sigh. 'He works too hard. Since his father died, he never stops.'

Teddy was about to ask when his father had died but suddenly realised that, as his wife, she should already know. She should know *everything* about him. She felt like an actor stepping onto the stage without learning the lines of the script first. 'Yes…he does work too hard.'

'Perhaps you will go on a honeymoon later, *si*?'

'Er…yes.'

Sofi cocked her head like an inquisitive little bird. 'You were not disappointed?'

'About the…er…honeymoon?'

'The wedding. There are not any photos, *si*?'

Teddy thought of that impersonal exchange of vows, the absence of emotion, the absence of a kiss. The absence of love. 'We didn't want a big fuss.'

'Me? I want a big fuss,' Sofi said. 'I want a white dress with a veil and a horse and carriage and three bridesmaids and a flower girl and a ring bearer. I want all my friends and family to be there and I want it to be in the cathedral with the bells tolling so all the people in the nearby villages can hear.'

Teddy felt a pang below her heart where the lid had slammed on her dreams. 'That sounds lovely.'

Sofi pushed her lips out in a little pout. 'I have to find a husband first.'

'You're rather young to be thinking about that.'

'I'm eighteen. My sister got married at seventeen. She has four children now. I don't want to be—how you say in English?—left on the shelf?'

Teddy thought of herself at Sofi's age, dreaming of the future. Imagining a handsome man sweeping her off her feet. It had all seemed so simple back then. Now she was married to a rich handsome man but he was counting the days until he could get rid of her. 'I'm sure you won't be left on the shelf, Sofi. You're far too beautiful.'

The young girl's dark eyes brightened. 'Do you think so?'

Teddy smiled. 'But of course.'

Sofi beamed back. 'I think Señor Valquez will be very happy. You are perfect for him. I didn't like his last lady friend. She was a—how you say?—a cold-hearted bitch? Do you know what she did to me the last time she stayed?'

Teddy knew she shouldn't be encouraging the girl to gossip but she wouldn't have stopped the impassioned speech for anything. 'No, what?'

'She told Señor Valquez I stole money from her purse.'

'Did he believe her?'

Sofi looked smug. 'No. He knows I would never do something like that. He trusts me. I am like a *sobrina* to him. A nice, *sí*?'

'Niece?'

'*Sí*, a niece.' A vigorous nod. 'He rescued me when I was living with a bad man who used to beat me. I owe him my life. I would never do anything to dishonour him.'

Teddy was starting to see Alejandro in a completely different light. It made the tight knot of resentment in her chest loosen a fraction. 'He's a good man to take such good care of you.'

'You love him very much, *si*?' Sofi said.

'I find it difficult to describe how I feel about Señor Valquez.' She hoped her cryptic answer was enough to satisfy the young girl.

'Maybe when you learn our language you will find the words, *si*?'

Alejandro was sipping a glass of wine in the salon when Teddy came in later that evening. She was wearing black trousers and an oyster-grey knitted cotton twinset with a string of pearls around her neck. Her hair was smooth and pinned back behind her head in her favoured style of neat chignon and her face was free of make-up apart from a shimmer of lipgloss. Her limp was particularly noticeable and he wondered if the long hours of travelling had caused her pain. He had tried to make the journey as uncomplicated as possible but still a twinge of remorse bit at him. She hadn't uttered a word of complaint but he knew it couldn't have been easy for her. Was she determined to be stoical about her situation? Show a bit of that charmingly named British phlegm?

'Did you have a rest?'

'Yes, thank you.'

He poured a drink and handed it to her. 'Sofi has been complimenting me on my choice of bride. I must congratulate you on acting the role of devoted wife so consummately.'

Her cheeks glowed with two spots of colour. 'I almost gave the game away. I suddenly realised I didn't know when your father had died.'

'Two years ago.'

'Is your mother still alive?'

'She lives in France. We're not close.'

Teddy bit her lip. 'We haven't sorted out how we met. How we came to…to fall…to get together.'

He watched as her cheeks went a shade darker. 'Let's stay as close to the truth as possible. We met briefly years ago. We met again recently in London and fell in love.'

Her forehead creased. 'You think people will believe that?'

He shrugged. 'It happens, or so I'm told.'

'But not to someone like you.'

Alejandro topped up his glass before he answered. 'People love to see a hardened playboy fall in love. It's our job to convince everyone for the next six months that it's happened.'

'What will I say when people ask me why we didn't have a proper wedding and honeymoon?'

'We tell them we wanted something intimate and private due to the recent death of your father and we'll take a honeymoon once the polo season is over.'

He handed her the platter of nibbles but she shook her head. 'Does your brother live here with you?'

'No, he has his own place half an hour from here but he spends a lot of time abroad playing the polo circuit.'

She worried her lower lip again. 'I can't help feeling I'm going to make a fool of myself over some detail I should know about you. Like where you went to school. What your favourite food is. What you like to do in your spare time…apart from rescuing street kids, which, by the way, you should have told me about.'

'It's not something I tell people, out of respect for Sofi and Jorge. I don't feel it is anyone's business if I help a couple of kids who needed a leg up.'

'All the same, you should've told me.'

'Why?'

She moved her shoulders as if she were shrugging off an unpleasant feeling. 'It would've made me feel a little less conflicted about coming here.'

'So you think because I've offered food and shelter to a couple of street kids I'm not quite the unfeeling Neanderthal you took me for?'

Her chin came up again. 'I would've appreciated a little background information, that's all. Apart from the stuff in the press, I mean.'

'I went to school in Buenos Aires until my high school years, where I went to boarding school in England,' Alejandro said. 'My father was keen for Luiz and me to have the experience of studying abroad. My favourite food is steak, medium rare. I don't have much spare time, but when I do I go hiking. Preferably alone.'

She nodded as if that made sense to her. Her eyes went to the contents of her glass but she didn't take a sip.

'What should I know about you?'

'I went to school in the village until I was seven, when my parents divorced. I went to boarding school after that.' She spoke in a flat monotone as if she were reading it from a pamphlet or talking about someone else entirely. 'My favourite food is chocolate. In my spare time I read or draw or wander about the garden, thinking.'

'What happened to your leg?'

Her mouth tightened momentarily. 'I fell off a horse when I was ten.'

'So you broke it…your leg, I mean?'

'My hip.'

'Must have been a bad fall.'

'It was.' Her expression gave him no clue. It was like trying to read a blank mask.

'How old were you when you had your first boyfriend?'

Her eyes skittered away from his. 'I can't remember.'

'That long ago, hmm?'

She drank from her glass before tossing the question back. 'What about you?'

Alejandro smiled at her countermove. He wondered if she had even had a lover. She didn't seem the type to be part of the hooking up culture. The more he saw of her, the more he thought she was the type of girl who would take her time before she committed to a physical relationship. Perhaps her hip injury made her shy. He hadn't met a woman yet who didn't have some fault to find with her body. Even the most beautiful of women struggled with how their bodies were perceived by others. How much worse must it be for her with an imperfection that was so obvious? Was that why she didn't play the fashion game? She didn't want to draw attention to herself in case people found her wanting.

'I had my first kiss at six and my first sexual encounter at fifteen,' he said to break the silence.

'That was young…'

'The kiss or the sex?'

Her blush deepened. 'I suppose you think I'm old-fashioned.'

'I haven't told you what I think.'

'You don't need to. I can see it on your face. You think I'm still a virgin, don't you?'

He held her look. 'Are you?'

Her chin came up again. 'No.'

He studied her features for a moment, noting her heightened colour and the pulse beating at her slim creamy throat. 'When was the last time you had sex?'

She made a choking sound and turned away. 'I'm not going to answer that.'

'Why not?'

Her arms went across her middle. 'Because this is a paper marriage so you don't need to know my sexual history any more than I need to know yours.'

'Mine is regularly documented in the press if you're interested.'

'I'm not.'

Alejandro watched her busy herself with her

drink, sipping it repeatedly as if she needed something to do with her hands. There was something about her quiet beauty that increasingly appealed to him. She didn't hide behind layers of make-up or designer clothes. She was simply presented, uncomplicated and yet deeply fascinating. Layered with secret desires he caught glimpses of now and again when she thought he wasn't looking. Her grey-blue eyes were intelligent and observant. Her manners were gracious and polished. She didn't speak down to the servants but treated them as equals. It would be so easy to overlook her in a crowd and yet she was the one that stood out the most when one took the time to get to know her. She wasn't worldly but she had an otherworldly air that was strangely alluring.

'Sofi reprimanded me for not carrying you over the threshold earlier.'

Her posture stiffened. 'I wasn't expecting you to.'

'But you were disappointed.' He watched the blush rise again in her cheeks. 'And at the ceremony too. It was remiss of me not to kiss you.'

She took a faltering step backwards, her eyes widening. 'I can assure you I'm not in the least disappointed.'

Liar. Of course she was disappointed. Damn it, *he* was disappointed. He had wanted to kiss that soft little mouth from the first time he had seen it pursed so tightly at him in disapproval.

He closed the distance between them, cupping her hot cheek with his hand, watching as her thickly lashed eyes rounded even further. He heard her snatch in a breath as her walking stick thudded to the carpet. Saw the tip of her tongue sneak out to moisten her lips. Felt his blood thicken in response to her closeness. To her light fragrance that made him think of old-fashioned cottage flowers. To the petal-like softness of her creamy-white skin, that was in such stark contrast to his olive tan.

They were standing toe to toe, her hips within a hair's breadth from his. He could feel the magnetic pull of male to female, the primal urge so strong it was overpowering. He put his other hand in the small of her back, gently pushing her until her breasts were touching his chest and her pelvis flush against his.

A rocket blast of lust fired through his groin. Heat exploded through his veins. Molten heat that made him swell and rise in anticipation. Need pounded. Thundered. Roared.

Her mouth parted on a breathy-sounding gasp. Her lashes came down as he lowered his head. Her breath danced over the surface of his lips, sweet and vanilla-scented. He touched his mouth to hers in a light brush of lips against lips, but as he pulled back her lips clung to his like a slip of satin did to a rough surface.

He went back for more, crushing her mouth beneath his as he gave in to the temptation to taste her, to devour her sweetness. His tongue stroked over the seam of her mouth and she opened to him with a shuddering sigh. He plundered the hot moist cave of her mouth, calling her tongue into sensual play with his, delighting in the way she responded to him with soft little mewling sounds. Her body pressed closer, her breasts flattened against his chest, her hips jammed against the swollen heat of his arousal, the erotic friction every time she moved making him wild with want.

He slid one of his hands into the silkiness of her hair, ruthlessly pulling it free of the elastic tie that had restrained it. It cascaded over her shoulders in a fragrant cloud as he deepened the kiss. He skimmed his other hand over her hip, then pulled her tighter to his pelvis, letting her feel the turgid outline of him.

Her tongue danced around his, shying away and then coming back at him with little darts and flicks. He was wild with his need of her. It was powering through him like an unstoppable force. Red-hot lust licked along his veins with breakneck speed, scattering every rational thought out of the way like gravel in a tailspin.

His hand found her breast, cupped it, palpated it as his mouth continued to feast off hers. She gave a soft whimper as he slipped his hand up under her cotton sweater, ruthlessly pushing her bra aside so he could feel her satin-soft skin. Her nipple was a tight bud between his fingertips. He circled it, round and round as he explored her mouth. Relishing in the little murmurs of approval she was making. Delighting in the way her body was as hot for him as his was for hers.

His hand reached for the fastening on her trousers but she pulled back from him as if he had thrown cold water over her. Her hands shook as she pulled her sweater back down over her breasts, her eyes shifting out of reach of his. 'I'm sorry...I—I can't do this...'

Alejandro sucked in a breath of disappointment so savage it shocked him. He prided himself on always being in control in any sexual encounter. But for a moment there he'd been out of control. His senses had been spinning so fast he had forgotten everything but the lust that was hammering through his system. His need was a pulsating ache in his groin. His mouth was warm with her sweet unforgettable taste, his hands tingling from the creamy softness of her skin.

Maybe it had been a mistake to ignore his physical needs for weeks on end. His last affair hadn't gone down well with his staff. It had been a mistake to bring the woman here. He usually kept his affairs for when he was away on business. It was less complicated that way. He had to admit the woman in question had been a little on the vacuous side. He'd taken some time out since but clearly his recent sexual drought had made him loosen his grip on his normally iron-strong control. He wasn't usually knocked sideways by a kiss.

What was it about Teddy that made him want to forget everything but the feel of male flesh sinking into hot wet female flesh and be damned with the consequences? Was that why he had kept his distance at the ceremony and in the car, somehow sensing that once he stepped over that boundary there might not be a way to turn back?

He schooled his expression into indifference but he wondered if she could see the glitter of primal desire he was sure was in his gaze as it met hers. 'I hope that more than made up for my inattention earlier.'

Her eyes moved away from his, her colour still high. Her lips were swollen from his kiss, her chin reddened from his stubble. Something shifted in his chest, a gentle tug, like a tiny child's hand pulling on the hem of its mother's skirt. She was about as far away from his usual lovers as innocence was to sin. Everything about her was different from his usual partners. Never had a lover pulled away from him.

He had the seduction routine down pat. A kiss, a caress, a look was all it took. It was a lowering thought but he had come to see sex as a right, an entitlement once he played his part of the game—the wining, the dining and the flattering comments. It was so easy and so predictable he had stopped thinking about it. He did it on autopilot. And he was good at it. He had a reputation for being irresistible. He had made himself that way. He wasn't allowing any woman to walk out on him again. *He* did the walking. He said when a relationship started and he said when it ended.

Teddy had stepped back when most women would have stepped forward but, rather than annoy him, it made him respect her. She was cautious by nature, measured in how she went about things. She would not be caught out by impulses or reckless decisions.

He watched as she gathered her hair back and made a makeshift ponytail using its length to restrain it. He wondered if it was her way of restraining her unleashed desires. Pulling herself together. Getting control.

He silently handed her the walking stick that had fallen earlier. She took it from him without meeting his gaze. 'I think I'll give dinner a miss if you don't mind.'

Alejandro squashed the bitter sense of letdown that swamped him. He would not admit he'd been looking forward to her company over dinner. That he enjoyed her smart tongue and quick wit. That he found it amusing the way she looked at him as if he had just swung down from a jungle vine with a club clutched in one hand. He would not admit he wanted to find out more about who she was and why she was so prim and starchy. He would not admit he wanted to find out more about her relationship with her father. About the dynamics of the father-daughter relationship that had led to a marriage with him when it was clearly against everything she believed in.

He didn't need her company.

Anyway, she would be gone in six months. He didn't want to get too used to having her around.

'Running away, Teddy?'

He saw the words slam into her like a blow. Her whole body stiffened and she seemed to brace herself before she turned around to look at him with that steady and arctic cool grey-blue gaze.

'It must surely be obvious to you by now that I can't run anywhere.'

Alejandro felt an unfamiliar twinge of shame. He wasn't a cruel person by nature, but he had to admit his words had been ill chosen. 'I'm sorry. I didn't mean to offend you.'

Her mouth was tightly set, such a contrast to how it had felt, soft and pliant, under his. 'What offends me is you thinking I'm so desperate for a man that I would consent to sleep with you. I don't even like you.'

He couldn't stop his top lip from curling. 'I guess that's why you slapped my face so hard when I kissed you just then.'

Her cheeks bloomed with hot colour and her

eyes flashed daggers of fire. 'It's not too late to do so.'

He glanced at her hands. Her left one was gripping her stick so tightly every knuckle was white. Her right hand was balled at her side, the fingers opening and closing as if she was preparing herself to take a swing at his face. He found himself wishing she would do it. He wanted an excuse—any excuse—to haul her back into his arms and kiss her senseless.

He brought his gaze back to her fiery one. 'Feel free.'

A battleground of emotions played out over her face. 'You think I'm so naïve as to fall for that ploy? If I slap you you'll just use it as an excuse to kiss me again.'

Alejandro smiled. 'And here I was thinking I wasn't predictable. You've got me all figured out, haven't you, *mi dulzura*?'

Her eyes flashed at him again. 'I will not be one of your playthings. I detest men who use women for their entertainment.'

'I would've made it fun for you too.'

Her colour rose sharply again. 'Do you ever think of anything but sex or work?'

'Food,' he said. 'It's right up there with the other two. Speaking of which, do you want me to send Sofi up with a tray? You might change your mind and get hungry later.'

The look she gave him told him she knew he wasn't talking about food. 'Thank you. But no.'

Alejandro watched as she limped to the door to leave. It was on the tip of his tongue to call her back. To apologise and start over. He had already apologised more in the short time he had known her than he had in his entire life prior to now. He hoped it wasn't going to become a habit.

The long warm spring evening stretched ahead of him.

Servants would surround him, but no one would make him laugh or stimulate his intellect. No one would challenge him…other than Jorge or Sofi, but that was different. They were still kids. It was adult company he craved. A beautifully spoken adult with Dresden blue-grey eyes that flashed and glittered like diamonds.

But no, he would sit at the long formal dining

table with its one place setting, the fruits of his arduous labour surrounding him: lavish wealth and luxury and food and liquor in abundance.

Somehow, he had never felt more dissatisfied than right now.

CHAPTER FIVE

TEDDY SHUT THE door of her suite and leaned back against it to get her breath. She could still taste the temptation of Alejandro on her tongue. She could still feel the warm caress of his hand on her breast. She could still feel the scorching heat of his groin as it had ignited a fiery need in hers. Her inner core was quivering with the unmet needs he had awakened and stoked with his devastatingly passionate kiss and blistering touch.

Their relationship was supposed to be formal. Hands off. Clothes on. Passion not only under control but stoically ignored.

She wasn't one of his floozies who could settle with a fling. For a night or two in his bed having bed-wrecking monkey sex.

She wanted to experience intimacy, respect

and mutual longing for connection, not just physically but emotionally and intellectually.

Why was he playing this seduction game? He didn't want her for her. She'd been thrust upon him and he was making use of her. The shallowness of it disgusted her. Sex was supposed to be sacred, a sharing of bodies that was much more than scratching an itch. She wanted to feel the romance of it—the shared pleasure of being with someone who understood her, respected her, wanted her. Not because she was available, but because she was the only one he wanted to be with. The only one he would ever want to be with.

She would never be that girl. Not for him. Not for anybody. Why would Alejandro want her? No one wanted her. Her father had made that more than clear by packaging her up as a deal not to be missed. *Ugh!* Why had he meddled in her life? Why hadn't he left her to get on with her life the best way she knew how?

She loved her work. It fulfilled her; it gave her a sense of purpose. She could cope with the loss of other dreams as long as she concentrated on her drawing. It stopped her thinking of the life she had dreamed of as an idealistic young girl. Marriage to a man she loved with all her heart and who loved her back. Babies—at least two, maybe three. A family like the one she hadn't grown up with. The stability she had craved for as long as she could remember.

It was pointless dreaming of such things now. Life had dealt her other cards. Cards that couldn't be put back in the pack and reshuffled and dealt out again. This was her lot in life. She had a lot to be grateful for. It was selfish and greedy to want more when so many people didn't get a chance at life, let alone a privileged one.

Once the six months were up she would have more money than most people would see in three lifetimes. Her father had amassed a fortune in property and stocks and shares. That money would provide her with enough capital to keep Marlstone Manor going and provide a home and security for her staff. She owed it to them to get through this period. She had no right to be distracted from her goal by a man who was far more attractive than he had any right to be. She wasn't a foolish teenager suffering a star-struck crush, tongue-tied and awkward when face to face with the object of her girlish fantasies. She was a responsible adult with people depending on her to do the right thing.

Teddy pushed away from the door and limped over to the lady's drawing desk where she had put her sketchbook and pencils. She turned through the pages, an acute sense of homesickness sweeping through her as she looked at the drawings she had done of the wisteria walk with the cheeky faces of fairies and elves peeking out from amongst the twisted vines and scented pendulous blooms.

She put her chin on her hand as she looked out of the window to the view of the gardens of Alejandro's villa below.

Somehow she didn't think she would find any fairy godmothers lurking about down there.

When Teddy came downstairs the following morning, Estefania, the housekeeper, informed her that Alejandro had been called down to the stables as one of his prize mares had been hurt by a kick from one of the yearlings as they were being led out to graze.

'I am not sure how long he will be, Señora Valquez,' the housekeeper said. 'He is waiting for the vet to arrive. You will like some breakfast, *si*? I can take it out on the terrace. It is Sofi's day off; otherwise she would be here to serve you. There is a sheltered corner out of the sun. Señor Valquez's father used to spend a lot of time there. He liked to be able to see the horses.'

Teddy was still getting over the shock of being addressed as Señora Valquez. It was silly of her to have not considered she would be addressed as such. Somehow she'd thought she would still be Teddy Marlstone. It was a little unnerving to think that title no longer existed. She was a married woman now, with a husband as handsome as the devil himself and twice as tempting.

'Breakfast on the terrace will be lovely.'

The sheltered corner of the terrace was a gorgeous spot with a curtain of wisteria that formed a scented grotto complete with a wrought iron table and chairs setting. A low hedge cordoned off the terrace, creating a tiered effect. The gardens were laid out below in stunning array, formal and neat like the grand stately houses of Italy and France. A marble fountain, with a Grecian goddess holding an urn, trickled musically below. The spring air was warm and fragrant and a light breeze teased the lime-green leaves of the wisteria like the breath of a ghost.

Teddy thought of Alejandro's father, Paco, a man tragically cut down by an accident. Confined to a wheelchair, unable to do anything for himself. Not even to bring food or drink to his mouth. How devastating for a man who up until then had enjoyed a full and active life as a polo player, as well as running an estate his forefathers had owned for hundreds of years.

She thought of his wife, Alejandro's mother, Eloise, who left when he was ten years old. From what Teddy had heard, Eloise had been unable to cope with the new circumstances of her marriage. Tied to a man who could no longer be a man. Who could no longer be a proper husband to her. That would have been a difficult heartbreak to face, a test of anyone's commitment to the words: *in sickness and in health.*

But what Teddy couldn't understand was how Eloise could have left her two young sons. What had led her to abandon them? And how had it impacted on them both? They were both notorious playboys who lived life in the moment. Alejandro managed every aspect of the business while Luiz travelled the world as a champion polo player. Both were driven to succeed, focused and ruthless in getting what they wanted. Had their father's accident and their mother's desertion made them distrustful of women? Wary of commitment? It would be doubly so for Alejandro who had suffered the ignominy of being jilted at the altar.

Teddy was finishing up her breakfast when she caught sight of Alejandro leading a horse with a bandaged leg. He was with a man who was carefully watching the horse's action, whom she presumed was the vet. They let the mare loose in a paddock, where she immediately bent her head to crop at the lush green grass. They stood at the fence with their backs to the villa, exchanging a conversation Teddy was too far away to hear.

She couldn't keep her eyes off Alejandro.

He was an inch or two taller than the vet and broader in the shoulders and leaner-hipped. His long strong legs were clad in blue denim jeans, which sculpted the taut contour of his buttocks. The bright sunlight made his black hair as glossy as a raven's wing, the light breeze lifting it now and again, which he combed back with a scrape of his hand.

Then, as if he knew he was being watched, he turned and raised a hand in greeting, a smile slashing whitely across the tan of his face.

Teddy's heart gave a little stumble…but then she realised it was all for show. He wasn't smiling because he was pleased to see her. He was smiling because the vet beside him would expect a man newly married to smile at his new bride.

Pushing down the jab of disappointment, she painted an answering smile on her face and waved back. But, rather than going back to the stables as she expected, the two men continued up to the terrace to join her.

Teddy knew she could hardly disappear inside, especially when Estefania came out with two more cups and a percolator of fragrant coffee.

'Dr Navarro will want to meet the young woman who has finally captured the heart of Señor Valquez, *sí*?' the housekeeper said with a broad smile.

Teddy's smile stretched a little further until her face ached. She wondered if the housekeeper knew she had spent the night alone in her bed and Alejandro alone in his. Or at least she assumed he'd been alone. Another little jab got her under the ribs. What if he had a lover amongst the many servants? She didn't like to think he would be the type of man to exploit the people under his employ but she knew such behaviour was common amongst the landed gentry. There were numerous young women about the estate. She had seen a couple of girls in the kitchen garden first thing that morning who looked to be in their early twenties. Would Alejandro fraternise with the staff or would he be a little more selective? Perhaps it was customary for men of his wealth and stature to do what they liked without censure.

As the two men arrived on the terrace Teddy rose from her chair, but somehow the foot on her bad leg got caught on one of the curved table legs and she pitched forward, creating a cup-rattling clatter in the process.

'*Dulzura*, are you all right?' Alejandro's strong grasp was suddenly there to steady her. His dark eyes were concerned and gentle as they met hers. 'You didn't hurt yourself?'

Teddy's pride hurt far more than her leg. She knew her face was fire engine-red. She could feel it blazing like a furnace. It reminded her of so many incidents throughout her childhood and adolescence where her clumsiness would make her the target of her father's cutting re-marks. Every time she stumbled she braced her-self for a barrage of stinging criticism. It was a programmed response she had never been able to shake off, even now with her father dead and buried in his grave. She made herself keep eye contact even though she longed to crawl away and hide. 'No, I'm fine. Sorry. I almost upended your coffee.'

A warm and tender smile tilted his mouth and her heart gave another little jerk in her chest. *He's pretending. Don't fall for it. He's putting on a doting husband show for his friend.* 'As long as you're OK.' His hand slid down her arm and captured her hand within his. 'I'd like you to meet a friend of mine. Ramon Navarro is the only vet I trust with my horses.'

The introductions were made and everyone sat down as Estefania served aromatic coffee and fresh rolls and preserves and a fruit platter that seemed to contain every stone fruit and berry and tropical fruit in the world. It was a cornucopia of colour and textures so beautifully arranged it was like a work of art.

Nice to be some people, Teddy thought as she reached for a plump strawberry. Did Alejandro dine like this every day? It made her cup of tea and tub of yoghurt seem rather pathetic in comparison.

'Alejandro tells me you've known each other from way back,' Ramon said once the first round of coffee was served.

'Yes…we met when I was sixteen.'

Alejandro reached for a velvet-skinned peach. 'Apparently I rudely ignored her. Not a good first impression, was it, *querida*?'

Ramon's hazel eyes glinted with amusement. 'Ah, but one must never go on first impressions, *si*? What is the saying in English about books and covers?' He cradled his cup in one tanned hand as he gave Teddy an appraising look. 'I always knew he would fall for someone like you.'

Teddy tried to smile but it didn't quite work. 'How do you mean?'

Ramon's smile was friendly and warm. 'Someone with intelligence. With depth.'

'Rather than beautiful, do you mean?' Teddy knew she shouldn't have said it. It sounded as if she was fishing for a compliment. It also sounded peevish. Childish and immature. Unsophisticated.

Which was exactly what she was, wasn't she?

She felt herself shrinking back in her chair, slumping like she used to do as a child when her father would give her that how-did-I-end-up-with-a-child-like-you? look. She wasn't a party animal. She wasn't even a party decoration. She wasn't a stunningly beautiful social butterfly able to mix in any company with ease. Was Alejandro's friend wondering what the hell

Alejandro was doing tying himself to such a nondescript woman?

'My wife has no idea of how beautiful she is,' Alejandro said. 'It's one of the things I adore about her.'

'Beauty is as beauty does, in my opinion,' Ramon said. 'But you have no need to be so modest, Teddy. You have a natural elegance that is captivating.'

While I'm sitting down, that is. 'Thank you.'

A silence was accompanied by the humming of a lone bee in the lavender-coloured wisteria blooms.

'Have you shown Teddy the hydrotherapy pool?' Ramon asked.

'Not yet,' Alejandro said. 'She's still getting over the jet lag. I haven't even shown her around the estate.'

'Water therapy would be good for her,' Ramon said. 'It will strengthen her muscles. Give her more stability.'

Hello? I'm still sitting here. 'You have a hydro-therapy pool?' Teddy asked.

'Alejandro had it installed for his father,'

Ramon said. 'Unfortunately, his injuries were too severe for any prospect of rehabilitation but at least he found being in the water soothing. It made a change from being in the chair or in bed all the time. Alejandro told me about your accident. You've had the limp a long time, *si*?'

'Since I was ten. My hip was totally reconstructed. There's nothing more I can do about my...gait.'

'You don't believe in miracles, Teddy?' Ramon asked.

Teddy had long ago stopped believing in miracles. Miracles happened to other people. The only dreams that came true for her were her nightmares. Wasn't she living one now? Married to a man who didn't want to be married to her. To a man who had to *act* as if he loved her. Who had to *pretend* to be concerned about her. Who had to *pretend* he thought her beautiful. The fact he did it so convincingly made a secret part of her want it to be true. The feminine part, the lonely-girl-no-one-wanted part *ached* to be found beautiful and interesting and lovable.

The foolish romantic part she'd thought she had locked away a long time ago.

This was all a game of pretence and the more lies they told the more complex the web of deceit became. She could feel it wrapping around her, choking her in its sticky prison.

'I'm a realist.' Her tone was bordering on sounding sullen but she didn't care. 'I know my limitations and I've accepted them.' Mostly.

Ramon leaned back in his chair, crossing one booted ankle over his thigh as he continued to study her. 'The human mind is a powerful tool in terms of healing. Chronic pain can be debilitating. People can spend years trapped in misery. But if you can break the cycle, be it with mindfulness techniques or other physical therapies, great results can be achieved.'

Teddy gave him a polite but stiff smile. How many times had she heard this lecture? The suggestion that her pain was somehow in her head annoyed the hell out of her. She had shattered her hip as a child. The horse had not only thrown her but trodden on her as well. She'd worn a black and purple hoofprint bruise for weeks on end. The bones had to be screwed and plated back in place. Her pain was real and it was constant. She had learned to live with it.

Alejandro put his hand on top of Teddy's where it was gripping the arm of the wrought iron chair and gently squeezed it. 'Forgive my friend, *mi amor*. He can't help himself. He's always on the lookout for someone to cure. Stick to your four-legged patients, Ramon. Leave my wife to me.'

Ramon gave a good-natured smile as he put his cup down in preparation to leave. 'At least you're in very good hands, Teddy. Alejandro can work the odd miracle himself when he sets his mind to it. You only have to look at young Jorge and Sofi to see that.'

CHAPTER SIX

ALEJANDRO STOOD WITH his arm around Teddy's waist as Ramon left to walk back to where he had parked his car near the stables. He could feel a band of tension running down from her shoulders to her lower spine. It was like holding an ironing board. Had his friend's well-meaning comments upset her? Her limp clearly embarrassed her, even though she had never tried to hide it from him. He had felt a rush of sympathy for her when she had almost tripped.

The long journey had obviously tired her. Her features look pinched and white, as if she was trying to cope with an elevation of pain. Had he asked too much of her by insisting she move to Argentina with him? He had convinced himself it was the only way to handle the situation. The best way. It was automatic for him to want to control things. He had been doing it since he was a ten-year-old child. Leaving things to chance was asking for chaos. For mayhem and panic. Someone had to be at the helm and keeping a watch out for unexpected surprises.

'I hope you weren't offended by Ramon. He means well.'

She stepped out of his hold and reached for her stick where it was leaning against the table. 'Not at all. I'm quite used to people telling me I'm imagining my pain.'

'That's not what he was—'

'Wasn't it?' Her eyes flashed ice and fire at him in equal measure. 'Is it what you think too? I suppose you're going to take me on as some sort of project, are you? Like one of your home-less kids or broken-down horses?'

He drew in a breath and slowly released it. She was hurt and she lashed out. Hurt and offended. She was exactly like one of his spirited fillies. Nervous and shy one minute, lashing out with heels and teeth the next. Even the way she tossed her head as she started for the French windows reminded him of a filly throwing her mane in disgust.

Was it his imagination or was her limp even worse?

He caught up with her and took her arm and turned her gently to face him. 'Is this about what Ramon said or something else?'

Her eyes were shimmering blue-grey pools. Deep and complex. 'You seem to enjoy lying. You do it so well. Telling your friend you adore me when the opposite is true. It's sickening.'

Alejandro raised his brows at her outburst. 'We agreed to act as if—'

'I hate the pretence,' she shot back. 'I can't lie convincingly. I'm rubbish at it. I'm bound to do or say something wrong and then people will talk. I'm surprised the servants haven't already started. I can't bear the thought of them speculating or gossiping behind my back. Making comparisons about me with all your previous lovers. Ugh! What are they going to think about our having separate rooms?'

He put his hands on her shoulders, cupping them against her slender frame. He felt her shiver as if his touch had triggered a reaction in her body. He felt the same kickback, as if an electric charge had come straight from her body to his. 'Are you saying you want to share my room?'

'Of course not!'

He smiled as he put a hand in the small of her back to bring her closer, watching as her eyes rounded and her soft mouth opened on a breathless gasp. 'You're right, *mi amor*. You're a terrible liar.'

Her hands were flattened against his chest but she didn't push him away. Her lower body was flush against his, the heat of their connection sending a river of lust through his blood. Want pounded in his heartbeat—a heavy insistent drumming he was sure she could feel through the soft flesh of her palms.

Her thick eyelashes lowered as her gaze slipped to his mouth. Her lips were slightly parted, rosy and pink and so youthful and unadorned. Had he ever kissed a mouth so sweet and tender? A mouth so innocent and yet so deliciously sultry once it lost its inhibitions.

He hadn't been able to get the taste of her out of his head. She was a mixture of honey and cinnamon and fresh milk. Her lips had been as soft as velvet, rich and warm and unforgettably responsive.

He brought his head down in slow motion, giving her the chance to move away if she wanted to. She didn't move. She stood in the circle of his arms, her breath dancing over the surface of his lips, making him want her with a potency that was shockingly primitive.

He touched down on her lips, intending to go lightly, but as soon as his mouth came into contact with hers a fireball exploded. Heat met heat. Want met want. Desire raced like a hungry flame in search of fuel. He crushed her mouth beneath his, all thought of tenderness lost in the firestorm of passion that blew up between them. Even before he moved his tongue forward to stroke for entry she opened for him, making a breathy sound of approval as he found hers and caught it up in a sexy slippery duel that made the blood pound even harder in his veins.

He pressed a hand to the dip at the base of her spine, holding her to the swell of his flesh, wanting her with an ache that throbbed in his groin to the point of pain. She moved against him with another soft murmur, her body leaning into his heat as if going purely on instinct.

He deepened his kiss, exploring the contours of her mouth, the warmth and sweetness of it tantalisingly addictive. Her tongue danced around his, darting away but each time coming back as if it couldn't resist the primal need to touch and taste and tease his.

He gripped her tighter as his body pounded with need. He could feel the tender shape of her mound against him, the barrier of their clothes somehow adding rather than taking away from the excitement. He rubbed the length of his shaft against her, groaning deep in the back of his throat as pleasure rippled through his body in waves. She made an answering sound, a purring sound of approval that made his insides contract with sharp delight. She felt so good against him. So soft and feminine and responsive, as if he and he alone unlocked her sensory heat. Her slim form fitted against him as if she had been custom-made for him. He could feel the gorgeous contours of her breasts pushed up against his chest, their softness against his hardness making him feel potently, powerfully male. He wanted her with an ache that reverberated through his body like an echo in a deep canyon. The very foundations of his body shuddered at the thought of taking her to oblivion with him.

He eased his mouth off hers, still holding her against him, his breathing not quite under control. 'This isn't the place to consummate our marriage, in full view of the servants. Let's go upstairs.'

She blinked as if awakening from a daydream. Then she pushed back from him and relocated her stick, gripping it as tightly as moments ago she had been gripping him. Her colour was high and her lips rosy and swollen from the pressure of his. But her eyes when they came back to his were spitting at him with livid heat. 'I suppose you think it's that easy. That *I'm* that easy. Poor little lame Teddy, gagging for a man to take her to bed. I've got news for you, Alejandro. I'm not *that* desperate.'

Alejandro held her vibrant gaze, watching as the blue and grey swirled in a kaleidoscope of fury. 'We could make this situation work for both of us. It's only for six months. Why not make the most of it?'

Her eyes narrowed to paper-thin slits. 'Make the most of me, don't you mean? I know how men like you operate. You have your fun and then you move on. Easy come, easy go. Find one of the servants to slake your lust with. I'm not that sort of girl.'

He sent his gaze over her in an indolent sweep. 'You were that sort of girl five minutes ago.'

Her mouth compressed to a flat white line. 'I could slap you for that.'

'Be my guest.'

She looked like a simmering kettle, standing there with her eyes blazing and her body shaking with impotent rage. She looked passionate and vital and, yes, beautiful. The whiteness of her skin contrasted with the red of her cheeks and lips made her look like a character out of a children's fairy story. Snow White or Sleeping Beauty in a towering temper.

'If I had fingernails I would scratch your eyes out.'

'Maybe you should grow them so you can scratch my back instead.'

Her cheeks glowed with heat, her mouth so tightly set her lips all but disappeared. 'You think this is funny, don't you? It's all a big joke having me here to amuse you whenever you feel like it. I'm a *real* person, Alejandro. I expect you don't meet too many of them in the circles you mix in. I'm not some stupid toy to be played with when the mood takes you.'

'Keep your voice down, *querida*,' Alejandro said. 'I don't want the servants to think we're having a tiff.'

Her eyes sparked with ire. 'We *are* having a tiff. If I want to argue with you then I'll damn well argue. That's what real couples do. They talk and discuss and have heated debates.'

'Here's another thing real couples do.' Alejandro took her by the shoulders again and pressed a hot, hard kiss to her mouth.

At first she made a startled sound of protest against his lips, but then, as if by magic, she softened on a little sigh and leaned into the kiss. Heat ran like fire from her mouth to his. He entered her mouth with a glide of his tongue, meeting hers in a combative tango that made his blood thicken him all over again.

She clung to him as if her life depended on the succour she was receiving from his plundering mouth. He put his hands on the slender curve of her bottom, holding her to the throb and pound of his body. She could deny it and fight it all she wanted but he knew she wanted him. He could feel it in every movement of her mouth against his. The way her tongue danced and flirted with his in a sensual swirl of activity. The way her breasts were pushed so tightly against his chest he could feel their hardened points pressing against him. He could taste her spiralling need in the sweet honey of her mouth. In the soft pressure of her lips as she nipped at his lower one in a cat and mouse caper that had his blood singing with delight.

The unleashed passion in her body stirred and stoked the roaring fire of his. Lust swelled and spread like an uncontrollable flame, whipping up a frenzy of want that had every nerve in his body screaming for release. The pressure built in his groin. Tight. Aching. Thrilling. Every corpuscle of his blood seemed to be quaking and shuddering in anticipation. Every muscle and sinew was taut with built-up tension, just waiting for the trigger point to explode.

He thought of how it would feel to sink into her warmth, to be surrounded by her feminine flesh, caressed and squeezed by the contractions of her body as she came. She wanted him as much as he wanted her. He could feel it. He could sense it. He could read it in every movement of her mouth against and within his. Her tongue was increasingly brazen, tangling with his in an erotic mimic of what they both wanted most of all.

He raised his mouth just enough to free her lips. 'Still want to deny what's between us, *mi amor*?'

She swept her tongue over her lips, briefly touching his lower lip with its tip. Her gaze was trained on his mouth, her lowered lashes shielding her eyes. Her breathing was heavy, her chest rising and falling against his, close to where his heart was thudding. 'You don't play fair.'

He brushed a tendril of her hair back from her

forehead with one hand while the other kept its position low on her spine. 'You're new to this, aren't you?'

He watched as her eyes moved out of reach of his, her teeth snagging on her lower lip in a gesture of uncertainty that touched on something deep inside him. How had he become so worldly and jaded that her reluctance to dive into bed with him was so refreshing? He was used to women beating a path to his trouser's zip. He wasn't used to shyness, to hesitancy or doubt. The women he dated took what they wanted from whomever they wanted it. He'd played the game with as much enthusiasm as them.

But this was different.

To Teddy this wasn't a game. And he realised with a strange little jolt that it wasn't a game to him, either. Making love with her would not be just another hook-up. It would not be just another sexual escapade in a hotel somewhere with someone he didn't expect—or want—to meet again.

This was different.

He was married to her. Legally married. They might not have had a big white church wedding but the certificate clearly stated they were hus-band and wife.

He would see her day after day for the next six months. Even if they didn't share a bed they would share other aspects of their lives. His work. Her work. Meals together, both in public and in private. Conversations.

He had never had someone enter the inner sanctum of his life. Not even his ex-fiancée had known everything there was to know about him. He didn't share confidences. He didn't talk about his work concerns. He didn't reveal his inner-most worries. His worries about his younger brother—whom he'd largely been responsible for raising—who spent so much time flying about the globe chasing the next game, the next woman, and the next thrill-seeking adventure. His worries over whether he was doing a good enough job with Sofi and Jorge.

Alejandro shouldered it all in silence because that was what he'd had to do since his father's accident. Having someone in his life, even for six months, was going to take some adjusting to. And if Teddy continued to be adamant they would not make their relationship a sexual one, it would still be as intimate as any he'd had before. He had never lived with a partner before. How soon before those clear observant eyes of hers saw the parts of him he liked to keep private?

Teddy's gaze came back up to his with defensiveness in every contour of her expression. In her upthrust chin, her tightly locked jaw. In her compressed lips. 'I know you think I'm an uptight prude. Maybe in some ways I am. But I can't change who I am.'

'I think you lack confidence,' Alejandro said.

'And I suppose you think you can help me gain some?'

'I'm sure of it.'

Her gaze flicked back to his mouth and he heard her draw in a deep shuddering breath. A pulse in her throat was beating like the heart of a hummingbird. Her tongue moved over her lips again, a nervous darting movement. 'I'm not ready to make that sort of commitment… I don't know you well enough.'

Funny, but not one of his partners had ever bothered getting to *know* him. All they had been interested in was the money he possessed. The experiences he could give them: expensive restaurants, jewellery, trips to exotic locations, evenings at the most exclusive parties and night-clubs. They hadn't wanted to know anything about him as a person. What he believed in. What values he held. What he feared and what he dreamed. *What he hoped.* He wasn't so sure he even knew some of those things himself. He had been so obsessed with getting the company back in the black that he hadn't had time to think beyond the next spreadsheet. He embraced work and pushed people away. It was a pattern he had fallen into. He was comfortable protecting and providing for the people he cared about but he wasn't so comfortable showing his emotions.

Alejandro brushed his bent knuckles down the curve of her cheek, watching as her eyes dark-ened. 'I'm not the easiest person to know. You sure you want to even try?'

She moistened her lips again before she gave him a tentative little smile that tugged on the spot deep in his chest. 'I guess I have six months, right?'

He leaned forward and pressed a kiss to the middle of her forehead. 'Indeed you have.'

CHAPTER SEVEN

SOON AFTER THEIR conversation on the terrace, Alejandro informed Teddy he had some emails to see to in his office. She wondered if he was giving her some space after their passionate kiss. Could he tell how confused she felt? How close she had been to offering herself to him? Her lips felt swollen and tingly and every time she ran her tongue over them she was sure she could still taste the hot salt of him.

He made her feel things she had no right to be feeling. The passion in his kiss had sent her senses into a screaming tailspin. She couldn't believe how brazenly she had responded to him. Pushing up against him, rubbing against the hot hard heat of him like a tigress on heat. She hadn't thought herself capable of such wanton behaviour. She hadn't thought of herself as a sensual person. But as soon as his mouth touched hers, her body took over her rational mind, urging her on with lustful longings she could still feel moving deep and low in her belly like a hungry beast on the prowl. The dragging sensation in her womb was an ache that made her aware of her femininity in a way she had never been before. Desire beat in her blood with a rhythm she could feel in every pore of her flesh. It thrummed and pulsed through her system insistently, making her feel restless and unsatisfied. Empty and hollow.

Her inexperience was so starkly obvious against his worldliness. She couldn't make up her mind if he was only interested in her because she was such a novel change from his usual partners. But the hopeless romantic in her wanted to believe he saw something in her that was unique. That he felt drawn to her because of who she was rather than what she looked like—that he wasn't put off by her limp or her reserved nature or her understated appearance.

He was a complex man—far more complex than she had first realised. He liked to give the appearance of hardboiled cynical playboy but he had other qualities. Much deeper, richer qualities the press knew nothing about. The fact he had taken in two street kids and provided a home for them and education and employment surely suggested he wasn't the shallow party-loving playboy the press made him out to be. He had invested in those young lives in a way that made Teddy feel deeply moved. He had used his wealth to make someone else's life better. Instead of spending it on himself and other worldly pleasures, he had given Sofi and Jorge hope and a future they could not have dreamed possible otherwise.

How much of his philanthropy did the press ever hear about? He obviously didn't bandy it about. He quietly got on with making a difference in people's lives, which made her feel all the more ashamed of how she had judged him. She had assumed he was ruthless and uncaring, arrogant and unyielding. But how could he be those things and care for others less fortunate than himself? The way his staff spoke of him revealed a side of him she longed to know more about. What made him so ruthless in business and yet so caring in his private life? He was focused and driven and yet he could take the time out of his schedule to see to an injured horse that clearly meant a great deal to him. Or spend time with a young boy, patiently helping him learn to read.

She had caught a glimpse of him in the study as she was heading back to her room. He had been taking Jorge through a lesson. She had stood outside the door, listening to the music of his voice as he spoke in his mother tongue. He had been patient yet firm in handling the young lad, who wouldn't have stood a chance out on the streets. Just who was this enigmatic man she would be married to for six months?

And would six months be enough time to find out?

Teddy used the rest of the day to get her bearings around the villa, memorising the layout so she didn't become disoriented. It was far bigger than she had imagined. Four storeys of grand opulence, each one decorated in a lavish style that spoke of enormous wealth. The beautifully appointed rooms were decorated in the finest fabrics and furnishings. But somehow she got the sense it wasn't a home. It was a beautiful showpiece, like an art collection someone had taken a long time to acquire. It had character but no soul. It was an exquisitely decorated shell.

Who would Alejandro ultimately share this beautiful home with? Would it ever ring with the sound of children's laughter? Had it ever been a happy home?

Teddy thought of Alejandro as a ten-year-old. How he must have felt when his father was critically injured. Seeing his father confined to a wheelchair with all the associated paraphernalia of a quadriplegic. Watching his mother walk out on him and his younger brother to find a new life in France. How had he coped with the devastation of losing not one parent but essentially two? His father would no longer have been able to do the things normal fathers did. He would need twenty-four-hour nursing care and support. How had Alejandro coped with the pressure of being the eldest son and heir? Knowing at such a young age he was the one who would have to take charge of the family business must have put an enormous burden on his young shoulders.

Teddy wandered into the library late in the afternoon, which overlooked the fields and the Andes Mountains beyond. Her gaze went to a photograph of Alejandro and his father and brother. It was sitting in a silver frame on the desk and had obviously been taken before his father's accident. She looked at the image of a handsome version of Alejandro standing with his arms around his sons, Alejandro on his right and Luiz on his left. The boys looked to have been around nine and seven. Paco had a rather stern expression as if he found being in front of the camera uncomfortable, but Luiz was grinning and cheekily pulling a face that crinkled up his nose. Alejandro's expression was also on the more sober side, which made Teddy wonder if he—like his father—had always been the one to take life a little more seriously than his younger brother.

There was another photo on the bookshelves along the back wall. Teddy was drawn to it like an iron filing was to a magnet. It was a picture of a stunningly beautiful woman holding a baby in her arms, with a toddler standing by her side, his little hand clutching the hem of her dress as if worried she might suddenly disappear.

So this was Alejandro and Luiz's mother. Could there be any better portrait of contented and happy motherhood? Eloise Valquez was dark-haired and fair-skinned with the sort of looks that reminded Teddy of a movie star from the golden age of Hollywood. Eloise was slender and glamorous with beautifully coiffed hair and perfect make-up and her dress looked as if it had come straight from a designer's studio in Paris.

What had happened to make that smiling, seemingly happy woman walk away from those two gorgeous little boys just a few years later?

Teddy looked at Alejandro's carbon-dark eyes, the way his forehead was puckered in concentration. She traced her fingertip over the serious little face, wondering what had been going on in his mind at the time.

'I see you've met the rest of the family.'

Alejandro's deep baritone sounding behind her startled Teddy so much she dropped the photo frame, but rather than land safely on the carpet it bumped the edge of the bookshelf on its way down. The sound of the glass cracking was as loud as a rifle shot. She bent down to retrieve the frame but a sliver of glass pierced her finger.

He was beside her within seconds. 'Have you cut yourself?'

She pressed her thumb against the end of her middle finger to blot the droplet of blood in case it fell on the carpet. 'It's nothing…I'm sorry about the frame. You startled me. I'll pay for a new one, of course.'

He took the frame out of her hand, giving it a cursory look before putting it to one side. 'Show me your hand.'

Teddy curled her fingers into her palm. 'It's just a pinprick. It's not even bleeding now.'

He held her gaze with that dark and intense determination she was coming to know so well. 'It might have glass in it.'

'It doesn't.'

He picked up her wrist with his long strong fingers and gently turned her hand over. One by one, he unpeeled her tightly clasped fingers until he came to the middle one with its tiny pearl of blood. He took out a snow-white handkerchief and daubed at the nick with care and precision, inspecting it for any trace of glass. 'It looks clean.'

'I told you it's nothing.'

His eyes meshed with hers and a wave of crackling energy passed between them like a wireless current. He was still holding her hand, his fingers sending the same fizzing shocks of electricity up her arm. His touch was so tender and yet somehow disturbingly erotic. Her body responded to him as if he had touched her intimately. She could feel the stirring of her core, the on-off pulse of need that moved through her flesh like a spreading fever. Her heart trebled its speed, the thumping so heavy she was sure he would be able to hear it.

She lowered her gaze from his and slipped her hand out of his. 'I'm sorry for being such a klutz. My father was always on about my clumsiness. I'll pay for a new frame. If you let me know where I can get it done I'll make sure it's as good as—'

'Forget about it.'

Teddy glanced back at his unreadable gaze. 'But it's a lovely photo of your—'

'I should've thrown it out a long time ago.'

She watched as he picked up the photo with its fractured glass cutting him off from his mother in a jagged line. He studied the image for a long moment, his expression inscrutable. Was he thinking of the day his mother had left? How he had felt? Had he been told she was leaving or had she just left without saying goodbye? Teddy wanted to ask but wasn't sure if he would appreciate her raking over old hurts.

'Your mother is very beautiful.'

He made a sound that could have been scorn or agreement; it was hard to tell which. 'She was always good in front of the camera. Still is.'

What did that mean? That Eloise Valquez hadn't been the perfect doting mother out of the sight of the lens? Had she been…cruel? Vindictive? Abusive?

He put the frame face down on the bookshelf. Teddy got the feeling he was closing a chapter of his life that had been open and raw too long.

'Do you ever see her?' she asked.

'Occasionally.'

'What about your brother?'

His mouth twisted on one side. 'Luiz plays the happy families game a lot better than I do.'

'You've never forgiven her for leaving your father.' Teddy didn't frame it as a question. She didn't need to. It was obvious what he felt about his mother. It was etched in every line and plane of his face, but most especially in his eyes. What had once been a child's bright galaxy of love shining there was now as empty as black holes in space.

He picked up a small marble ornament off the bookshelf and turned it over in his hands. 'She shouldn't have married him in the first place.' He put the ornament down and picked up another one—a brass one this time—rubbing his thumb over the smooth round top as he added, 'It was either marry my father or be disinherited from her family.'

Teddy frowned. 'Disinherited? But why?'

He gave her a look. 'You can't guess?'

She pulled at her lower lip with her teeth. 'Oh...'

'She was pregnant with me.' He put the ornament down with the same note of finality he had the photograph, a frown settling between his brows. 'A fact for which she could never quite forgive me.'

Teddy's heart contracted. Had his mother *told* him he was unplanned? Unwanted? Or had he picked it up in the subtext of his parents' relationship? 'Surely she didn't blame you? But that's ridiculous! You didn't ask to be—'

'It was different with Luiz...but only for a while.' The frown was still heavy between his eyebrows. 'There are some women who should never be mothers. They don't have the right temperament.'

Teddy thought of how dearly she longed to be a mother. The nurturing maternal gene was almost *too* strong in her temperament. She wished she could turn it off so she didn't have to live with the empty sadness of knowing she might never hold her own child in her arms. She couldn't walk past a pram without a wistful peep inside.

She went to mush over kittens and puppies. She couldn't imagine not loving a baby she had given birth to, even if the circumstances weren't quite right in terms of the relationship with the father of the child. 'Was she…abusive?'

He looked at her for a long moment before answering. 'It depends what you mean by abuse.'

Teddy swallowed. 'Did she hit you?'

His smile didn't belong on his mouth. It clashed with the bitterness in his eyes. 'The sting of words lasts far longer than a slap.' But then the bitterness dulled as he added gently, 'But maybe you know a little about that too.'

She could see no reason to hide it from him, even though for years she had been playing at happy families too. It was the thought of someone—*him*—understanding how hard it was to love a parent who was largely unlovable. 'My father wanted a boy. That was his first disappointment in me. The second was that I wasn't beautiful. And the third was I wasn't a natural athlete.' She gave him a little grimacing smile. 'That's how I ended up with this hip. Along with everything else, I wasn't up to my father's standard as a rider. I was barely at the level of riding a fat, elderly Shetland pony. He put me on a spirited newly broken two-year-old Arab. Not a good result, as you can see.'

He frowned darkly. 'He *forced* you to ride it?'

Teddy remembered the butter churn of nerves in her stomach as her father insisted she mount the prancing horse, which had seemed as high as a bell tower. Her hands had been shaking as she took the reins and her legs had felt like two columns of jelly as she put her feet in the stirrups. She had been terrified she might wet her pants. 'There was a certain amount of pressure, yes. My father wasn't one for leading strings. It was sink or swim with him. I sank.'

Alejandro's eyebrows lowered even further, pinching together over his eyes. 'You were lucky you weren't killed. What was he thinking? What sort of father does that to his own child? Your safety should've been his first priority.'

Warmth spread through her chest at his anger on her behalf. Audrey and Henry had been too frightened for their jobs to say much upfront but they had supported her in the background as she convalesced. Audrey had told her in later years she and Henry had decided it was better to stay quiet and stay so they could look after her than to speak up and be dismissed and leave her to the mercy of new staff. It had been a wise decision, for Teddy couldn't imagine how much harder her childhood would have been without their love and support.

'He told me during the last weeks of his life about his childhood. It explained a lot about his parenting style. He was brought up by a tyrannical father who beat him mercilessly if he so much as stepped a toe out of line. My father was obsessed with perfection because, as a child, his safety depended on it. I chose to forgive him. Little did I know he'd planned this.'

'This being us?'

'As mounts go, you're hardly an overweight elderly Shetland pony, are you?' As soon as she said it she felt a hot blush crawl over her cheeks.

His eyes glinted as a slow smile spread across his mouth. 'Is that what you were looking for in a husband? A benign Shetland pony sort of guy?'

'I wasn't looking for a husband.' *I already have one I don't know how to handle.*

'You don't want a family one day?'

Teddy gave him an eyeball-to-eyeball stare, hoping it would disguise her secret longings. 'Do you?'

He lost the smile and exchanged it for a grim flat line. 'It's something I used to think about a lot.'

'But not now?'

His indifferent shrug belied the tense set to his features. 'Family life is hard work. I've seen that first-hand. Life throws up curve balls and not everyone's up to the task of dealing with them.'

'But you're already doing it...bringing up a family, I mean. Jorge and Sofi are your family, or at least they see you as theirs.'

He gave a lip shrug this time. 'Maybe.'

There was a long silence.

'What was your father like before the accident?'

He picked up a quill pen from the desk near the window, brushing the fronds of the feathers through his fingers. 'He was a good man.

Steady, hardworking. A little on the serious side at times, but he had a lot of responsibility on his shoulders. My grandparents hadn't managed the business well, due to a number of factors. But, to be fair, some of them were out of their control.'

He put the quill down and met her gaze. 'It was ironic that the very qualities my mother was attracted to in my father were the ones that bored her witless a couple of years into their marriage. His steadiness became boring. His seriousness became irritating. She wanted fun. Nightlife, parties. New experiences. Other lovers. They argued a lot, which made my father all the more serious and steady to counter her unpredictable mood swings and rages. He couldn't win.' He let out a long sigh. 'And then the accident happened.'

Teddy saw the pain of remembering that time on his face. The vertical lines between his nose and mouth seemed to deepen in front of her eyes. His eyes took on a haunted depth like the inside of a cave where dark and menacing shadows lurked. Somehow she suspected it was a place he only rarely and very reluctantly visited.

'My father wasn't expected to live through the first forty-eight hours but somehow he did. I often wonder if he wished he hadn't. He never said anything but that was his way. He dealt with what was handed him. Stoically. Grimly.'

Like father, like son, Teddy thought. 'It must have been a terrible time for you and Luiz.'

'I did what I could to protect him from what was going on. He was only eight. Intensive care units are not the place for young impressionable children.'

'But you were only ten.'

A ghost of a rueful smile flitted across his mouth. 'I was old enough to understand things were going to be very different from now on. If my father had died my mother would never have coped with single parenthood. We would've been handed over to relatives before he was cold in his grave. I sat by his bedside and prayed for him to make it. I *willed* him to live. I was determined to keep our family intact.'

'But then she left.'

His hands were holding the back of the leather chair behind the desk, his knuckles showing white against his tan. 'She lasted longer than I thought she would. Six months. She would have left at three but her lover was still living with his wife. Once he was free she was off.'

'What did she say to you? How did she explain it to you and Luiz?'

He took his hands off the back of the chair. 'She said she was going on a little holiday. That she needed a break from looking after our father. That she'd be back before we knew it.'

Teddy's mouth dropped open. Her heart felt as if it were being crushed between two bookends, knowing the bewildering despair he must have felt as a young boy. 'She *lied* to you?'

His expression showed very little of the bitterness she could sense in his soul. His face was a mask which cloaked his emotions. 'It was worse for Luiz. I knew she wouldn't be back. He didn't. I didn't have the heart to tell him for a couple of months. He used to run to the window of whatever room we were in when he heard a car coming up the drive and press his face up to the glass. It was like a knife twisting in my gut every time I saw his face fall in disappointment. In the end, I had to tell him.'

'How did he take it?'

A flicker of pain flashed through his gaze. 'He didn't believe me. He got angry. He played up at school. Started wetting the bed. Threw tantrums. But then, after a while he seemed to come out of it. He threw himself into sport. Anything that involved competition. He trained hard and played hard. He's still doing it. Don't get between him and a win. He would rather die than lose.'

Like someone else I know, Teddy thought. 'Did your mother ever come back to visit you?'

His face was hard as marble. 'She came back two years later. Her lover had left her for another woman by then. She was at a loose end and wanted to take Luiz back with her to France.'

Teddy's heart contracted again. 'She didn't want you to go too?'

His look said it all. 'My father refused to give her custody of Luiz. She would've been charged with kidnap if she'd taken him out of the country. He knew she wouldn't fight him over it. She didn't really want the responsibility of a child, even her favourite child. She soon found another lover, and another after that. She's with a man who's only two years older than me now. God knows how long that will last. She doesn't know the meaning of the word commitment.'

'She's taught you and Luiz well.' Teddy hadn't meant to say the words out loud.

The silence that followed was damning.

She bit her lip. 'I'm sorry. That was insensitive of me.'

He let out a rough-edged sigh. 'No. It's true. We're both wary of commitment, Luiz even more so than me. At least I can last a couple of weeks with someone. He's known as the king of one-night stands. I worry about him. But that's hardly new. I've spent the last twenty-four years worrying about him.'

'You're a good brother, Alejandro, and a wonderful son,' Teddy said. 'Your father must have been so proud of you.'

He moved from behind the desk to stand in front of her. He tipped up her chin to mesh his gaze with hers. 'Behind that starchy façade you're quite a sweet caring little thing, aren't you?'

Teddy knew he was hiding behind mockery in the same way she hid behind her cool mask of composure. It was a default setting they had in common. They were both wounded and ultra-careful about letting people get close. 'It's not wrong to care about people, especially people you admire and trust.'

His eyes moved between each of hers in a back and forth study. 'So you admire and trust me, do you, Teddy?'

She held his gaze even as her heart skipped a beat at the dark intensity in his. 'I think you're a man of principle. A man of honour. You have strong values and you stand by them, no matter what.'

His slanted smile was sardonic. 'You mustn't be reading the papers. Haven't you heard I'm a ruthless, hard-living playboy with a heart of stone?'

Teddy pressed her hand to his chest where his heart beat like a steady drum under her palm. Her body was so close to his she could feel her breasts brushing the front of his shirt. The fronts of her thighs were close enough to touch the powerful muscle-packed strength of his. Heat coursed from deep inside her, moving through her flesh in a swirling hot tide that left no part of her unaffected. 'The papers don't always report the truth. Only their version of it.'

His hand cupped her cheek, his eyes still studying hers with that same probing intensity. 'Are you sure you want to be this close to me?'

'I've been safe so far, haven't I?'

His gaze went to her mouth and her stomach gave a little flip turn as he brushed her lower lip with the pad of his thumb. 'How long do you think that's going to last?'

Teddy felt the tingles of his touch deep in her body. His eyes were so dark she could barely make out his pupils. His mouth was tilted in that worldly smile that made her insides quiver. But her old companion—self-doubt—reminded her he was not in this for keeps. He was looking for some fringe benefits to make the situation between them more palatable. He didn't want the servants to gossip. What better way to put a stop to speculation than by bedding his new bride? He might have stronger values than she'd first thought but he had physical needs too. How soon before he lost interest? A month? A week? A night or two? How soon before he found someone else who was as athletic and perfect as him?

She stepped back from him, holding her stick for support. 'I have no interest in complicating an already complicated situation.'

'Sensible girl.'

Was she? If she had been sensible she wouldn't have agreed to come here with him. Entering the lion's den was not a sensible thing to do. Spending time alone with him was unwise.

Falling in love with him would be the biggest mistake of all.

CHAPTER EIGHT

THE NEXT FEW days passed with Teddy spending most of the time drawing while Alejandro worked on the estate. He spent a lot of time outdoors but he burned the midnight oil as well, for she saw the light in his office well into the early hours of the morning. They shared an evening meal most days but she was conscious of not spending too much time alone with him. Lingering over the table with a glass of wine was asking for her guard to be lowered. Risks to be taken. Kisses to be repeated.

Her body was aware of him in ways she was doing her best to ignore. Which was why she decided to resort to the pool in the sun-drenched gardens to work off a bit of her restlessness. The hydrotherapy pool was enclosed in a cabana next to the main pool but she decided against using it. The rails and ramps reminded her too much of her rehabilitation when she was a child. The agonising sessions with her impatient father looking on, demanding she try harder. The frustrated physical therapists who knew their jobs were on the line if she didn't improve according to her father's standards. Her own disappointment at not being able to fully recover. Of being different. Disabled.

The only swimming costume Teddy had was a black one-piece. She wrapped herself in a bathrobe and made her way to the pool, where Sofi had very kindly placed a towel on one of the sun loungers. The secluded pool shimmered in the bright sunlight. The scent of summer flowers teased her nostrils as she slipped out of the bathrobe and carefully made her way into the water. The water enveloped her body like liquid silk, caressing her limbs, making her feel weightless and free in a way she hadn't felt in years. The only stroke she could do, and not very well, was breaststroke. It was the only way she could keep her head above the water. Being tossed in the deep end when she was a child hadn't made her feel very confident as a swimmer. But here, with the sun shining and the birds twittering in the shrubs nearby, she could enjoy the simple pleasure of moving through the water in a more or less rhythmic fashion.

Teddy was doing her tenth lap when she heard a firm footstep on the flagstones. She looked up to see Alejandro standing there watching her. He was dressed in his work clothes—denim jeans and a cotton shirt that was open to the middle of his chest, revealing the dark tan of his skin and the sprinkling of masculine hair. Beads of perspiration shone on his forehead and she could see wet patches beneath his armpits. He looked strong and vital and intensely, unapologetically male.

Her body responded to his presence with a shiver that seemed to start inside and move outwards over her flesh. His gaze travelled over her breasts, lingering for a moment on their puckered points before moving back to mesh with her gaze. 'Mind if I join you?'

'It's your pool.' Teddy moved to the side. 'I'm getting out, in any case.'

'No need to run away.' He unbuttoned the rest

of his shirt, his eyes never once leaving hers. 'There's enough room in there for two.'

She gulped as his chest glistened in the sunlight. The ridges of his abdomen made her fingers twitch to touch him to see if he was as hard as he looked. She swallowed as he lowered the zip on his jeans. The rasp was loud in the silence. His work boots and socks were next, hitting the flagstones with a thud she felt deep in her core. Her eyes were drawn like magnets to the proud heft of him concealed behind black underwear. He stood with his thighs slightly apart, strong and hairy and muscled. She swallowed again and made a grab for the railing but he had already anticipated her move and covered her hands with both of his. The warmth of his touch on her cooler flesh felt like a searing brand. It sent a river of heat through her blood, making her heart pick up its pace as his gaze locked on hers.

He entered the pool, the action shifting the water so it lapped over her breasts as if he had reached out and caressed them. 'It looks like you could do with some tuition.'

Teddy pursed her mouth. 'How nice of you to point that out.'

'I didn't mean it as criticism.'

'Didn't you?'

His eyes kept holding hers as he came a step closer. Close enough for her to stop thinking of moving away. She couldn't move away if she tried. The jolt of awareness, of longing, was like the sting of a stun gun. She was trapped by her own traitorous desire.

'Are you sure you should be doing breaststroke with your hip the way it is?'

'I don't like getting my head wet.'

He studied her for another long beat. 'I could help you with that. I taught Jorge to swim. He was terrified of deep water but now he swims like a fish.'

Teddy was so used to failure she couldn't bear the thought of having him witness her struggle to meet his expectations. He was built like an Olympic athlete. How could he possibly understand how hard it was for mere mortals like her to get from one end of the pool to the other?

'Thanks for the offer but I wouldn't want to waste your time.'

'I wouldn't push you beyond your capabilities. I'd make sure you were confident first.'

It was hard to know if they were still talking about swimming. Something about his intensely dark gaze made her think of making love with him. That strong, powerful body moving within hers, making her feel alive and electric with sensation. She could feel the tingle of her breasts as his gaze moved over them again, her nipples pushing against the wet fabric of her swimming costume. His hands were still covering hers, holding hers, imprisoning hers. She could feel the latent strength in his hands. Imagined them touching her all over her body…her breasts and her belly and in between her thighs. Touching her intimately. Stoking the fire of passion that was simmering inside her even now.

Teddy watched the slow descent of his mouth towards hers. Felt her heart jump as his lips touched down against hers in a firm kiss that sent a shockwave of heat through her. His tongue moved along the seam of her mouth, nudging it open and taking possession in a smooth gliding thrust that made the backs of her knees tingle. She leaned further into the kiss, into him, the feel of his erection against her belly pouring more combustible fuel on the fire that was raging inside her. Her arms went around his neck, holding his head in place, her mouth returning his kiss with a rush of passion she had no idea she possessed. Her breasts felt swollen and tight against the hot hard plane of his chest.

His hands went to her hips, holding her to his pelvis, inciting the fire inside her into an uncontrollable blaze. His teeth played with her lower lip, teasing and tugging, his tongue salving the sting with sexy raspy glides. Shivers coursed down her spine like a runaway firework, a cascading spiralling sensation that made the hairs on her head stand up and tingle at the roots.

He brought a hand between their bodies, touching her between the thighs in a gliding stroke that followed the seam of her body. The sensation was electrifying…hot bursts of need exploded inside her flesh. She pushed herself against his hand, wanting more. Wanting him.

He nudged the edge of her costume away and stroked her again, this time slipping a finger inside her, gently exploring her, letting her get the feel of him before going deeper. She whimpered at the contact, the hot sexy glide of his finger awakening a powerful need that was building with every stroke against her flesh. His mouth smothered her cries as she rose on a pitch of ecstasy that was like being on the top of a cresting wave. She fell over and tumbled into an abyss of pleasure, as if she were being bathed in royal silk. Her flesh hummed. Her body sang.

She stood clinging to his body to remain upright after such a powerful onslaught. Shocked at her response to him. Shaken by the power of it.

'You're so responsive...' He said the words against her mouth, making it part speech, part kiss.

Teddy couldn't believe it was her hand reaching down to stroke him through his underwear but her earlier shyness had gone. She wanted him to feel what she had felt. She needed to feel his response to her. He was thick and strong, pulsing with need as she shaped him. She saw the way his jaw clenched as if he were controlling the urge to let go. It made her movements bolder. More brazen and uninhibited. She slipped her hands down past the elastic waistband and moved her fingers over his blunt tip, rolling and caressing until she could feel the pressure against her hand as he fought for control.

Alejandro covered her hand with his, stilling her movements. 'The problem with pool sex is protection.'

'Oh…'

He kissed her mouth in a long slow kiss, finally easing back to look at her a little ruefully. 'I should have started this somewhere I could finish it.'

Teddy looked at the strong tanned column of his throat, her shyness suddenly returning. 'Do you want to? Finish it, I mean?'

He tipped up her chin, a frown pulling at his brow. 'How can you be in any doubt of that?'

She tugged at her lip with her teeth. 'I'm not your usual type.' *How do I know if this is just a convenient fill-in for you? While for me…this could be the only chance of experiencing...* She pulled away from her straying thoughts. What was the point of thinking about love? Men like Alejandro didn't fall in love with girls like her. He didn't fall in love, full stop.

He searched her features for a long moment. There was a lot going on at the back of his gaze. She wondered if he was mentally sifting through his past lovers, looking for a match that came anywhere near her. 'No.' He let out a breath and gently held her by the shoulders. 'You're completely different.'

Which was bad...wasn't it? Teddy couldn't say the words out loud. But she could hear them hovering in the silence.

'Why do you doubt yourself so much?' His frown was still in place, his gaze focused on hers in a gentle rather than stern fashion.

She gave a little shrug under the warm cup of his hand. 'My father wasn't big on compliments. I never seemed to do the right thing. It started when I was born a girl instead of the boy he wanted. Then I wasn't cute and chubby and blonde but long and skinny and brunette. I wasn't sporty. The list was endless.'

His hands on her shoulders squeezed against her flesh in a soft reassuring motion. 'He was a fool. You should never listen to the opinion of a fool.'

Teddy closed her eyes as his mouth came back to hers in a kiss that had *To Be Continued* in its every erotic movement. Her insides quivered as he scooped her up in his arms and carried her up the steps of the pool. She was dripping wet but he barely paused long enough to gather a towel.

In no time at all they were in the privacy of his bedroom, a masculine suite that was a world away from the soft femininity of hers. He laid her on the bed and, stripping off his wet underwear, joined her in a sexy tangle of limbs.

Teddy stroked her arms up the silken steel of his back and shoulders. The feel of him lying over her was a blessed weight but she wanted much more. Her inner core was aching for his full possession; the needs he had awakened and temporarily satiated were back with a hunger that was even more urgent and ravenous. She could feel it clawing at her as his mouth came back down to hers, his tongue mimicking the act of making love with such blistering accuracy she felt the pressure building like an ache.

He left her mouth to move down her body, taking her swimming costume with it. His mouth found her breast, caressed it hotly with his lips and tongue, circling the nipple, teasing it with soft little bites that made the base of her spine melt like molten wax. He moved to the other breast, subjecting it to the same exquisite torture until her back was arching like a sensuous cat. Just when she thought she could take no more he upped the ante. He trailed his mouth down between her breasts, dipped his tongue into the shallow cave of her belly button and then went lower.

Teddy clutched at the bedcovers to anchor herself as his tongue gently parted her. The sensations were so soft at first she thought it would not amount to much. But then he changed the pressure, varying it, reading her body, gauging her reactions to tailor his sensual assault to maximum effect. The sensations built to a crescendo and then were triggered into a cataclysmic explosion that shook her body like a rag doll.

When he came back to her mouth she could taste her saltiness on his lips. He deepened the kiss and she played tag with his tongue, gaining confidence with him as the passion she could feel in his body rose to fever-pitch. He dealt with the issue of a condom with a deftness she could only imagine came from extensive experience.

But right now she didn't care a blink for any of his other partners. This was between them.

Here and now.

And right here and now she could feel the sheathed length of him at her entrance. She could hear his low deep murmur of reassurance as he slowly eased her apart to enter her. She could hear her own soft gasp as her body resisted him at first, but then, with his gentle coaxing and slow progression, she welcomed him fully. The flood of pleasure at receiving him moved through her body like the rush of a warm wave. It rippled over her as he began to move. Slowly at first, not too deep, letting her get used to the length and breadth of him.

Teddy was swept up in a whirlwind of mind-blowing sensations. The sensuous glide of his hands on her breasts and on her belly. The way he kissed her with such tenderness and yet such heady passion made her feel like the most special, most beautiful girl in the world. The way his tongue played with hers, teasing it into a playful duel that made her lower body ache for release all over again. He moved to caress her between her thighs with his fingers, that final stroking enough to send her flying into a sea of pleasure. Her whole body shook with the power of her orgasm, heightened by the hard thick presence of him moving with such rhythmic motion. The contractions of her body triggered his release. She felt every powerful pump of it as he emptied. She felt him shudder in her arms, his long tall body tensing and then completely relaxing in the afterglow.

There was a long silence.

Alejandro eased up on his elbows to look at her. 'I didn't hurt you? Go too fast for you? Rush you?'

Teddy stroked her hands down the length of

his back to the base of his lower spine. 'It was wonderful. You were wonderful. I never realised it could be…like that.'

He brushed a stray tendril of hair away from her forehead, his eyes dark as night as they held hers. 'You haven't done this much, have you?'

She bit her lip and lowered her gaze to his Adam's apple. 'You can tell?'

He bumped up her chin with his fingertip. 'Don't be ashamed of that, Teddy.'

'It wasn't by choice.' She let her shoulders go down in a sigh. 'I wasn't the most popular date. Who wants to party with a girl with a limp?'

He brushed a fingertip from her cheekbone to her chin. 'It's not your stick that puts people off but your shtick.'

Teddy gave a self-deprecating smile. 'Yeah, well, a girl's got to have something to fall back on when her looks don't amount to much.'

His frown came back. 'I wish you wouldn't do that.'

'Do what?'

'Put yourself down all the time.'

Teddy watched as he rolled away to dispense

with the condom. 'I'm only repeating what others have said. I've heard them. I've been hearing it all my life. *She's not very pretty, is she? Good Lord, is that Clark Marlstone's daughter? Doesn't take after her mother, does she?'* She pulled the covers over her nakedness, suddenly feeling exposed, like a soldier crab without its shell. 'You thought it yourself, didn't you? When you came to the house that first day. I saw it in your eyes. You were shocked at my appearance.'

Alejandro's jaw tightened. 'Because you wanted me to be, didn't you? You dressed like a bag lady that day because you're so used to being judged you thought you'd get in first. It's a defence mechanism. I understand it, Teddy. I really do. You've been hurt too many times. Your confidence has taken one too many hits. But I want you to stop doing it.'

Teddy gathered her knees close to her chest, wrapping her arms around them, creating a barricade. A new shell. 'And do what? Pretend I'm six foot tall with perfect endless legs and blonde hair and big baby-blue eyes like your ex? Like that's going to work.'

He stood looking at her for a long moment. But then he let out a whooshing breath and came back to sit beside her on the bed. He stroked a finger up and down the back of one of her tightly interlocked hands. 'You *are* beautiful, *querida*. Don't let anyone tell you different.'

She met his gaze and for a moment she felt beautiful. His gaze was warm and dark and surprisingly tender. His fingers unpeeled her hand and he lifted it to his mouth, kissing each fingertip as his eyes held hers. 'You have the most beautiful eyes I've ever seen.' He outlined her mouth with a lazy fingertip. 'Your mouth is beautiful. So soft and sweet.' He leaned forward to press a kiss to her lips. It was a tender kiss and yet passion was there in the undertow. She felt it when his tongue briefly brushed her lower lip. Shockwaves of feelings rushed through her like a fizzing current. The sensual power he had over her was mind-blowing. How could she ever resist him now she had lowered her guard? Even more worrying—how would she live without him once their marriage came to its inevitable end?

He eased back to look at her. 'Your body is beautiful.'

'I have scars.'

'Where?'

'On my hip.'

He angled his head to look at her hip. 'That tiny white line is a scar? I didn't even notice it.'

He bent his head and kissed his way up her thigh from her knee until he came to the fine white line. His tongue grazed her skin, accelerated her heart, and rushed her breathing. He gently pushed her back down on the bed, coming over her in a gentle press of male flesh on female, stirring her senses into a heated frenzy all over again.

Teddy linked her arms around his neck as his mouth came back down on hers. Her fingers delved into his hair, threading through the dark thick strands as he kissed her senses into a tailspin.

He cupped her breast in one hand, his thumb moving over the engorged nipple in a back and forth motion that made her insides quiver with need. He was hard again and pressing urgently against her thigh. She brushed her hand over him, heard his groan against her lips. 'I want you.'

She lay back as he looked down at her with those dark as coal eyes. They heated her flesh to boiling point. She could feel the warmth rising in a hot tide that flowed from her core. 'I want you too.' *I want you now. I want you tomorrow. I want you forever.*

Teddy closed the door on the thoughts like a host did on unwelcome guests. *Here and now.* That was what she had. That was what she would enjoy because all too soon it would be over.

But she would have her house and her inheritance. That was what she was here for. Nothing else.

Because nothing else was on offer.

Alejandro watched as Teddy slept during the early hours of the morning. She was curled up like a contented kitten, her cheek resting on one of her hands, the other lying on his chest, right over his heart. Her legs were entangled with his; her small feet looked tiny compared to his, her

toenails unpainted, but for all that neatly manicured. Her skin was pale as milk, untouched by
the sun, with no tan lines whatsoever. Her hair
was loose and tousled and was spread in a dark
cloud over the pillow. It smelt of winter violets.

He had considered sending her back to her
own room after they had made love but somehow he hadn't got around to saying the words. It
had felt right to hold her, to watch as she drifted
off to sleep, to feel her body snuggle up against
his as if she belonged there.

Her inexperience had affected him more than
he wanted to admit. Touched him. Made him
think of making love instead of having sex.
Made him feel something he normally wouldn't
feel. He *always* separated emotion from sex. He
focused on the physical because that was all he
ever wanted from a partner. But making love
with Teddy wasn't just about base needs being
met. Every time he touched her, kissed her,
moved within her, he felt as if she was giving
something of herself to him. It was unlike his
other encounters. He couldn't think of a single
one where he had felt more in tune with a wom-

an's body. Her lack of experience had not just been a novelty but something he found strangely moving. She had given not just her body to him but also her trust. She responded to him with a passion that seemed to surprise her as much as it delighted him.

He frowned as he absently played with the strands of her hair. Sex was supposed to be sex. He could keep his feelings separate when each encounter was much the same. Seduction had become a game for him. One he never lost. He had women whenever he wanted for however long he wanted them. He made the rules and made sure no one flouted them.

But somehow the game had changed. The goalposts had shifted. The stakes had gone a little higher. He had set out to win the war but had foolishly ignored the battle.

This was no longer about a plot of land that should never have been sold. This was about a man and a woman from two different worlds and two different perspectives coming together and finding perfect physical harmony. Walking away when the time was up might not be as simple as he had initially thought.

You could ask her to stay longer.

The thought slipped under his guard like a torch beam shining light beneath a locked door, illuminating an array of possibilities he normally never allowed himself to entertain. A long-term marriage, not the debacle his parents' had turned out to be, but one that blossomed and matured and improved with age. Having children to pass his wealth along to as his forebears had done. Watching them develop and grow from infants to adulthood, supporting them and loving them above all else. Making the villa a home instead of a rich man's castle, a place where children could laugh and play without fear of reprimand, unlike his and Luiz's childhood because the needs of their ill father had always taken precedence.

A home.

But Teddy had her own home. One she had given up her freedom to secure. She was unlikely to sacrifice Marlstone Manor to spend the rest of her days in Argentina. His mother had tried to adjust to living in a foreign country and look how that had so dismally failed. It was a huge change to move from the Northern hemisphere and live in the Southern. The seasons were all back to front. The weather was different, the language, the culture—everything was far from all that was familiar and sometimes attraction, let alone love, wasn't enough.

Alejandro wasn't prepared to risk it. Their relationship was for six months. That was all both of them needed to achieve their mutual goals.

Teddy drew in a deep breath and nestled closer against him as she released it. The waft of her breath skated over his chest like a teasing feather. He could smell the sweet scent of her hair and skin mingled with the scent of his, that and the aroma of recent sex. The musky fragrance seemed to mock him. *This is what you wanted. You wanted to prove you could have her. But in six months she'll be gone because at the end of the day it isn't you she wants. You're nothing but a means to an end. You could have been anybody and she would still have agreed to marry you to get her home back.*

He frowned as he looked at her sleeping features. He had married her when he had said he would never marry anyone. He had slept with her the whole night when he had never done so with anyone since his ex. What was next? What had been Clark Marlstone's intention? That Alejandro fall in love with his daughter, knowing she had only married him for financial gain? She would be gone as soon as the property was safely in her possession. Any foolish notion he harboured of continuing their marriage would be asking for the same humiliation he'd experienced a decade ago.

So what if the sex was the best he'd had in ages...probably ever? He was letting feelings cloud his judgement. He had to keep his eye on the prize. The land would soon be back in his hands and that was all he had ever wanted.

He would allow nothing or no one to come before it.

CHAPTER NINE

WHEN TEDDY WOKE the next morning Alejandro came in with a tray with her breakfast on it. Her heart gave a funny little jolt against her ribcage when he gave her a crooked smile. 'Sleep well?'

She pushed herself upright and brushed back her tousled hair. 'Like a baby.'

Something moved over his features as he set the tray on the side of the bed next to her. There was a knot of tension in his jaw. His brow momentarily furrowed. But it was gone by the time his gaze reconnected with hers. 'I got a call from my brother. He's flying home for a few days. He's keen to meet you.'

Teddy took the cup of tea he passed her and cradled it with both hands. 'Will you tell him we're—?'

'It's none of his business.'

He moved to the window to look at the view

outside. The muscles of his back and shoulders were showing tense through the light cotton of his shirt as he thrust his hands in his trouser pockets.

'Are you close to him?'

'He's my little brother.'

'Some brothers hate each other's guts.'

'Not in this case.'

Teddy wondered if he allowed anyone close enough to share the responsibilities he carried. Did he indulge his younger brother? Giving him the freedom he had missed out on because of the responsibilities that had been thrust upon him? From what she had heard from snippets from Sofi and Estefania, Luiz was a charming flirt with a wild reputation. Did Alejandro wish he too could be free to live his life without the burden of other people's welfare on his shoulders?

Last night she had been as close to him as anyone could physically be and yet he was still a stranger to her emotionally. Was he regretting it? Regretting the intimate boundaries they had crossed? Their marriage would not be so easily dissolved now it had been consummated. Was he worried she would beg him to keep her on indefinitely? That she would pressure him to make their marriage a real one in every way possible? Did he think her so desperate for affection she would beg him to keep her when she'd known from the start marrying her was the ultimate sacrifice a playboy of his stature could make?

She looked down at the contents of her steaming cup. 'Last night doesn't change anything.' She heard him turn around but didn't look at him. 'When the time is up I'll leave as planned.'

The silence was broken by the sound of a horse whinnying from one of the fields below.

'Why did you agree to sleep with me?'

Teddy adopted a nonchalant expression. 'You asked nicely.'

He gave her a look. 'I mean it, Teddy. Why?'

She fiddled with the handle of her teacup. 'I wanted to know what it felt like. I've only slept with one partner before and it wasn't the most pleasant experience.'

His brows snapped together. 'He didn't force you, did he?'

She shook her head. 'No…nothing like that. It was while I was at art school. He was a classmate. A friend…or so I thought.' She took a breath and continued. 'I found out later he only did it to win a dare.'

'That's despicable.'

'I thought so too.'

He came back over to the bed and sat on the edge to take one of her hands in his. 'So you've never been with anyone since?'

'No.'

His dark gaze studied hers for a long moment. 'You said last night doesn't change anything. Does that mean you don't want to continue sleeping with me?'

'Is that what you want? To sleep together, I mean…for as long as we're together?'

His expression was unreadable. 'It makes sense, wouldn't you say? There are few wives who would want their husbands straying.'

Teddy gave him an arch look. 'I would imagine most husbands wouldn't be too keen on their wives straying, either.'

His inscrutable gaze measured hers for another beat. 'Is that what you'd do? Find someone else?'

She let out a long breath. 'No. I know the vows we said were only for show but I'm not the type of person to break a promise even if it's a fake one.'

His thumb moved over the back of her hand in a stroking motion. 'Last night was…' he paused as if searching for the right word '…special.'

Teddy couldn't quite keep the cynicism from her tone. 'The best sex of your life?'

A frown pulled at his brow but he didn't pause in his stroking of her hand. But neither did he answer. She wasn't sure if he was annoyed by her question or considering the right way to answer it. Was he comparing her performance with his harem of past lovers? Was she a stand-out? If she was, it was probably because she was so inexperienced, so gauche and so clumsy.

She looked down at their joined hands, the dark tan of his skin against the pale cream of hers. His fingers felt strong and warm, soothing and yet arousing. His thigh was close to hers and even though the sheet provided a barrier she could still feel the tempting heat of his body. Her insides quivered at the memory of how those hard muscled thighs had felt against hers last night. Her inner core contracted as she thought of how it had felt to welcome him into her body. 'I wasn't fishing for compliments.'

His lips moved in the vestige of a smile as he gave her hand a gentle squeeze. 'I know you weren't.'

'*He* said that…the guy I was telling you about.' She screwed up her mouth. 'I didn't believe him, of course. It might have been my first time but I wasn't so naïve that I fell for that.'

The silence continued for another beat or two.

Teddy lost herself in his molasses-dark gaze; the smouldering heat of it triggered a pulse deep inside her body. She could feel her body stirring, and then pulsating with an insistent beat. She could see the same reaction in him. The flaring of his pupils. The way his gaze dipped to her mouth and back again. The way his thumb kept stroking the back of her hand in a sensual rhythm that evoked another contraction in her core.

He lifted his other hand and gently brushed the back of his knuckles down the curve of her cheek. 'You might be sore after last night.'

'I'm not.'

'Are you sure?'

Teddy surreptitiously squeezed her legs together but he must have felt the movement against his thigh nearest hers for his expression took on a rueful twist even though she thought she'd done a good job of hiding her wince.

He sent his knuckles down beneath her chin this time. 'I'd like to show you around the stables some time.'

Teddy swallowed a lump of panic. 'I'm not very good around horses. I'd rather admire them from a distance.'

'You won't be in any danger while you're with me.'

I'm already in the biggest danger. 'You're not expecting me to ride one?'

'Not unless you want to. I can teach you if you'd like. I taught Jorge and Sofi.'

'I'll pass.'

'I'm a good teacher, or so I've been told.'

Teddy was in no doubt of it, given her body was still humming from all he had taught her last night. 'I'm a bit of a slow learner. It might take more than six months to teach me. What then?'

He held her look for a beat as if he were mentally processing the possibility. 'It won't take you that long. It's all a matter of confidence.'

'I'll think about it.'

He continued to hold her gaze in an assessing manner. 'Sometimes facing the things that frighten you the most is the only way to get control of your fears.'

Teddy gave him a wry look. 'Does that mean the next time I bring roses into the house you won't toss them in the nearest bin?'

A muscle tightened in his jaw. 'Fine. If you want roses then ask Estefania to get you some.' He rose abruptly from the bed. 'I'm not sure when my brother will show up. He sometimes texts beforehand, but not always.'

'Why do you hate roses so much?'

He pushed a hand through his hair, dropping his hand back by his side as he released a rough-sounding sigh. 'They were my mother's favourite flower. They still are, or so Luiz tells me. My father indulged her passion for them. He planted half an acre of them. He imported every variety. He didn't care how much it cost. But it wasn't enough to keep her. No amount of roses was ever going to do that.'

Teddy frowned as she mentally surveyed the villa's gardens. 'I didn't see any roses outside.'

He gave her a look that spoke volumes.

'You got rid of them? *All* of them?'

He drew in a breath. Released it again. 'The day my father died I ploughed them into the ground.'

'But is that what he wanted? Did he ask you to—?'

'There was no point keeping them once he'd gone.'

Teddy thought of all of those gorgeous roses crushed, destroyed, decimated, all those bruised and broken petals bleeding their perfume into the soil. 'It was wrong to do that.'

His expression hardened. 'Do you know how good it felt to bury those wretched plants? They represented everything I detest most. Disloyalty. Cowardice. Betrayal.'

She pressed her lips together, unwilling to engage in a heated argument over something that caused him so much pain. It was another reminder of how much he was coming to mean to her. He valued the same things she did. It was what she admired so much about him. He was brave and strong and loyal to those he most cared about.

A tiny flicker of hope fluttered in her chest. Would he come to care about her too? Did he already? Sometimes she thought she saw something in his gaze…a thoughtful look, a look that lingered longer than it needed to, as if he were thinking beyond the time frame of their arrangement. Or was that her wishful thinking taking over? Was she imagining the tender look that came into his dark eyes whenever she winced with pain from her hip?

She changed the subject rather than torture herself with hopes that had no business occupying her thoughts. 'I'll make sure I'm always prepared for your brother's arrival.'

He gave a grunt as he moved to the door. But on the way past he noticed the drawings Teddy had been working on and stopped to look at them. 'Are these yours?'

'Yes.'

He picked up her sketchbook. 'Do you mind if I take a look?'

'Go for it.'

Teddy watched as he turned over page after page, his brow furrowed in concentration. After a while he put the sketchbook down to look at her. 'You're very talented. I had no idea how talented.'

'My father thought I was wasting my time.'

'Yes, well, he would, wouldn't he?' Alejandro seemed to be speaking to himself as he leafed through the sketches she had left on the desk.

'Did you know him at all?'

He put the drawing he was holding down on top of the others. 'I ran into him at various functions over the years. Apparently he and my father had met while my father was in England on a student exchange. They continued their friendship as they had mutual business interests. But

I'm not sure my father still considered him a friend after he realised how he had been duped over the sale of the land.'

'He didn't speak of it to you?'

Alejandro picked up one of her pencils and tested the sharpness with his fingertip. 'I was only ten at the time. My father did his best not to burden me with things he thought I was too young to understand. But I understood all right. I knew how he'd been tricked and I swore I would do whatever it took to bring about justice.'

'Did my father know you felt that way?'

He put the pencil down and met her gaze. 'I may have made the point on the odd occasion when our paths crossed.'

Teddy chewed at her lower lip. 'I still don't understand why he did what he did. I don't think he even *liked* my second cousin. Why would he as good as hand everything to him instead of me?'

'Because some people like to play games with other people's lives,' he said. 'They get a sick sense of enjoyment out of causing trouble.'

She let out a long sigh. 'I guess you're right...'

He came back over to her and eased her chin

up with his finger, meshing his gaze with hers. 'He's not worth worrying about, Teddy. He might have been your biological parent but he wasn't a father to you any more than my mother was a mother to me.'

She gave him a barely-there smile. 'I know…'

He leaned down and, cupping her face in his hands, pressed a soft kiss to her mouth. 'I won't let him win this, *querida.*'

I think he already has, Teddy thought as the door closed on Alejandro's exit a moment or two later.

Teddy stood next to Alejandro as they watched Jorge and a more senior stable hand working one of the polo ponies in the training arena a few days later. Alejandro had given her some background on how the family business had developed. His grandfather had made money through other investments, including vineyards and olive groves, but as a young man Alejandro's father developed a passion for breeding and training and selling polo ponies after he had spent time in England as an exchange student. Since Alejandro had taken control of the business he had sold ponies to European and Middle Eastern royalty, and his vision was to build an eco-friendly polo resort on the land Teddy's father had bought off his father. Teddy could hear the passion in his voice as he described the resort he had dreamed of since he was a child. His love for the horses and his concern for their welfare was something else that was clearly obvious.

'A good polo horse must be ridden every day,' Alejandro said. 'We start slowly because it's important for the horse to be relaxed until he learns about the game. See how Jorge is riding and playing with long reins? That means when the chukka is finished, the rider should be able to put the reins on the neck of the horse and it will automatically walk back to the pony line.'

'They're beautiful animals,' Teddy said, silently envying the way Jorge was riding seemingly so effortlessly.

Alejandro glanced down at her. 'Would you like to try sitting on a quiet mare? I'll lead you around so you get the feel of it.'

'I don't know...' She bit her lip as she looked

at the gorgeous horse the stable hand was bringing over to her.

Alejandro stroked the mare's glossy neck and
the horse rubbed against him as if in bliss. 'This
is Pepita. She's too old to work up much more
than a trot. I'll help you get on.'

Teddy stood with her nerves jangling as Alejandro put his hands on her waist from behind.
'Relax, *querida*. I know you're nervous but I'll
be here all the time. Up you go. Go on. You can
do it.'

It wasn't the most graceful mount but neither did she tumble off the other side. Her legs
gripped the leather of the saddle and her hands
clutched at the mare's mane. The mare didn't
fidget or fuss. She stood perfectly still, apart
from her head as she nudged Alejandro and blew
her nostrils at him in search of a treat.

'All right so far?' he asked.

'I think so…'

'You're doing great.'

He began to lead the mare, checking to see
if Teddy was keeping her balance. Surprisingly, she did. Her thigh and abdomen muscles

switched on and after a few metres she felt herself relaxing into the saddle, becoming one with the horse's movements instead of feeling like a cumbersome burden.

Alejandro smiled up at her. 'You're a natural. In no time at all you'll be riding like a pro.'

Teddy thought that was very generous of him but couldn't help glowing at the compliment all the same. He didn't press her to try a trot; instead he said they would take it one day at a time, building on her confidence until she was ready for the next step.

She wondered if he was taking the same approach with her in the bedroom. The last few nights he had shown her how much of a sensitive and attentive lover he was. Not rushing her, letting her find her comfort level with him. The way her body responded to him constantly surprised her. It made her feelings about him all the more confusing. She was determined not to fall in love with him but her body had other ideas. It was madly in love with him. Feverishly so. It thrummed with delight whenever he touched her. Even when he looked at her in a certain way she felt a frisson pass through her flesh.

Alejandro helped her down off the mare and walked back with her to the villa, one arm around her waist, which she tried to tell herself was not just because his stable staff were watching. The strong band of his arm sent tingles of awareness through her body. 'Do you fancy a swim?'

I fancy you, Teddy thought. 'Sure.'

It took her a moment to realise he was leading her straight to the sheltered pool area. She stalled mid-stride. 'I need to change into my bathers,' she said.

He gave her a glinting look. 'No, you don't. We can swim naked.'

'What if someone sees me?'

'*I* want to see you.'

'I mean someone else…the staff or—'

'My staff know we sleep together in the same bed. They'll hardly think it strange for us to swim together naked. Anyway, they know me well enough to keep their distance.'

'I suppose you've done this with past lovers

hundreds of times.' Teddy hadn't meant to sound so miffed but his past was so colourful compared to hers. Would she ever feel as sophisticated and poised as her peers? Why couldn't she be as casual about sex as everyone else was? As *he* was? Why did she have to dream of having him fall in love with her the way she was rapidly falling in love with him?

He stopped to turn her in his arms. 'We've both brought baggage to this relationship. It doesn't mean we can't have a good time while we're together.'

While we're together.

Did he have to keep reminding her of how temporary this was?

Teddy shivered as he set to work on the buttons of her cotton shirt. One by one he undid them, his eyes locked on hers with smouldering intensity. Quivers of longing speared through her as he released her bra, his warm hands cupping her, stroking her, fuelling her desire. She did the same to his shirt, pressing her mouth to his sun-warmed flesh, tasting the salt of him, trailing her tongue down his sternum. He gave a little shudder as her hands went to his waistband. He stepped out of his jeans and underwear, the afternoon sun casting his toned body in a golden glow. She couldn't keep her hands off him. She stroked him all over, holding the swollen length of him in her hands, delighting in the weight of his arousal.

They moved to the steps of the pool but, before Alejandro could submerge himself, Teddy stalled him with a hand on his chest. 'Sit.'

He raised his brows ever so slightly but his dark eyes glinted in anticipation. 'If you're about to do what I think you're about to—' He let out a colourful expletive as she took him in her mouth, sucking him in without preamble. She felt him jolt back in delighted surprise, heard him groan deeply as she continued her intimate ministrations. He made a vain attempt to stop her by placing his hands on her shoulders but she was on a mission to deliver the same mind-blowing pleasure he had given her.

And she succeeded.

He gave a whole body shudder and quickly pulled out to spill. It was shockingly arousing to watch him ejaculate. To think that she had brought him to that point with her lips and tongue made her body pulsate with want.

He took a ragged breath before sending her a scorching look. 'Of course you know what comes next.'

Teddy felt a delicious tingle race up and down her spine. 'Me?'

He reached for her, switching places so she was the one sitting on the edge of the pool, her thighs spread. She tilted her head back as he caressed her with his lips and that wickedly clever tongue. She was beyond caring if anyone was watching from the villa. Right at that moment she didn't care if it was being beamed live around the globe. The only thing she cared about was the sensations that were rippling through her body. Her orgasm hit like an earthquake, sending shockwaves of pleasure through every pore of her flesh. She gave herself up to it, letting it take her further. Another orgasm followed, even more intense than the first. It shook her body until she was limp and weightless.

Alejandro lifted her into the water to stand

in front of him, thigh to thigh. He kissed her slowly but thoroughly, leaving no corner of her mouth untouched. She felt the rise of his erection against her belly and reached between them to caress him. 'Are you on the Pill?' he asked.

The question wasn't an unreasonable one but it still surprised her. 'Yes, to control my cycle. Why?'

He looked into her eyes for a long moment. 'We're being exclusive, yes?'

She gave him a self-deprecating look. 'It's not like I have any other offers on the table.'

He stroked a fingertip down her cheek. 'You're doing it again. Putting yourself down. You're the most responsive and passionate lover I've ever had.' He paused for a moment before adding, 'I sometimes wonder if I ever truly enjoyed sex until I met you.'

Teddy felt the last of her defences crumble. What hope had she ever had of keeping her heart out of this? He had stolen it the first time he'd seen her limp and didn't flinch away in disgust. 'It feels good for me too.' It sounded hopelessly inadequate but she didn't know what else to say.

I love you wasn't quite appropriate, given the circumstances. But he trusted her enough to have sex without using protection. Did that mean he wanted their relationship to not only be exclusive but ongoing? Was this a sign of a deep yearning to get as close as he could to her? Or maybe that was her wishful thinking on overdrive again.

'It will get better and better.' He turned her so she was facing the steps, holding her against him so she could feel the heat and weight of his erection from behind. 'Are you comfortable with me this way?'

'Yes.' *Oh, yes!* Teddy felt him against the cheeks of her bottom and another frisson trickled over her flesh. He entered her gently, letting her get used to the position, but once she was comfortable he didn't hold back. He drove into her with increasing vigour, each thrust sending her senses into ecstatic overload. The friction became even more pleasurable, the dominant male position somehow targeting her most sensitive spot with just the right amount of pressure. The tension rose in her body until it was at snapping point. She hovered there in that final moment, suspended on a high wire before pitching headlong into paradise. She gasped and cried, shuddered and shook, clinging to the edge of the pool to anchor herself from the storm until it slowly abated.

His release followed in a series of deep hard thrusts, the clutch of his hands on her hips as he drove himself over the edge sending another wave of delight through her body. He cut off a wild cry as he came, the sound torn from his throat sounding so primal and so utterly male it made her shiver all over again.

He held her in place as he fought to get his breathing back under control. There didn't seem any point in speaking. Their bodies had said all that needed to be said. Teddy relaxed against him, letting her head tilt to one side as his lips nuzzled the side of her neck below her earlobe. She gave a little shiver as his tongue found her ear. 'That tickles.'

He moved his mouth down over her shoulder, licking, stroking, his teeth gently tugging at her flesh until she squirmed in delight. 'I love the feel of your skin. It's like the petal of a flower.'

Teddy turned in his embrace and linked her arms around his neck, her look playfully pert. 'A rose?'

He gave her a twisted smile. 'Let me guess… they're your favourite flower?'

She smiled back, loving the closeness, the way he was holding her and looking at her with that tender expression in his dark eyes. She had never felt more desirable or beautiful than at that moment. 'I've always loved them. We have a huge garden of them at Marlstone. I spend a lot of time there sketching.'

He kept his hands on her hips, gently holding her against him. 'What do you love about them?'

Teddy unhooked one of her hands from around his neck and used it to stroke his stubbly cheek. 'I love that they're both prickly and thorny and yet the blooms are so soft. They smell so divine. Hot and spicy, or subtle and romantic, or just simple and fresh after a shower of rain.'

His gaze held hers for a long moment, before he let out a long sigh as he traced his index finger down the slope of her nose. 'You're right.'

'About what?'

'I shouldn't have got rid of them.'

Teddy brushed her thumb pad over his lower lip. 'You could put new ones back in. Create a whole new garden that's nothing like the old one.'

There was a beat or two of silence.

'Would you help me?'

She looked at him blankly. 'Me?'

'Why not you?'

She pulled at her lower lip with her teeth. What was he asking, exactly? His expression wasn't easy to read. It was as if he had deliberately veiled it. 'I'm not a horticulturist or anything but it's the wrong time to plant roses. You should do it in the winter. That's what…eight months away?'

'I know that, but you could help me choose the varieties. You could draw a plan for the layout of the garden. With all the groundwork done ahead of time it would be relatively simple to implement once winter comes.'

Teddy didn't want to think of where she would be once winter came around. 'I'd be happy to help if you think I'm the right person for the job.'

He smiled and brought her closer as his head came down to kiss her. 'You're perfect.'

CHAPTER TEN

ALEJANDRO LEANED ON the top rail of the fence of the riding arena as he watched Teddy ride Pepita in a slow but steady trot a few days later. Teddy was sitting beautifully, riding the mare's rhythm without any sign of nerves or fear. She even smiled at him as she came round to his side of the yard. It was in moments like this that he realised how much he cared for her. *Really* cared for her. His emotional muscles were stiff and atrophied from lack of use but each time she smiled at him he felt them loosen a little bit more, become more agile.

He became aware of his feelings for her in the same way he had become aware of her quiet beauty. Gradually. It crept up on him, catching him off guard in little moments: a certain look of hers, her shy smile, her tinkling bell laugh at something cheeky Jorge said. The caring concern she had for Sofi when Sofi had woken during the night with period pain. The way she spent hours with Jorge, with some of her picture books, encouraging him to read them with her to build his confidence. Even giving him a set of pencils, charcoal and a sketchpad and giving him tips on drawing.

She helped around the villa, arranging the flowers for the table for Estefania, putting little touches about the place that made the villa feel more homely. Casual colourful cushions in the sitting room to soften its austere atmosphere, opening curtains and pulling up blinds to let more sunshine in the formal rooms, indoor plants, little posies of flowers in every room to bring the freshness of the outdoors inside.

She encouraged Sofi and Jorge to eat with proper manners, showing them which cutlery to use and how to make conversation with someone they didn't know. She did it all with patience and grace, complementing the efforts Alejandro had already put in.

She had spent hours working on the rose garden plan, talking to the gardeners and showing them the websites where the list of varieties were listed for ordering when the time came.

He worried that she would be overtired from all her efforts but each day she seemed to be stronger. Her limp was obviously not going to go away, but he was sure it was less noticeable, or maybe it was less noticeable to him.

He smiled as she came around again to his side of the fence. 'You're doing so well, *mi dulzura.* Before you know it you'll be cantering.'

'I don't know about that.'

Alejandro helped her out of the saddle, not because she needed it now but because he looked for any opportunity to touch her. To hold her in his arms. *To protect her.* The yearning to do so was so strong he wanted to tell her then and there. But rushing in was not his way now. He quite liked keeping the knowledge that he loved her secret for a little while longer. He suspected his staff already knew. And Sofi had already told him she couldn't wait until he and Teddy had babies so she could help with them. The thought of raising a family with Teddy was like discovering a treasure that had been long buried. Children to make the villa a home again. Laughter and love and lives intertwined. How could he have thought he didn't want those things? He wanted them but only with Teddy.

He wasn't going to tell her here. Not in front of his stable hands. And not in front of his brother, who had texted he was on his way. No, he would take her away for the weekend to somewhere private. Indulge her like a princess; tell her he wanted her to stay with him forever.

He kissed her softly on the mouth. 'I got a text from my brother. He's five minutes away.'

Her face fell. 'Oh, no! I'm filthy. I smell of horse and hay and—'

'You look beautiful, *querida*.'

She looked at him in distress. 'But I wanted to be prepared. What will he think of me? My hair all mussed from under the helmet and my clothes all dusty and dirty.'

Alejandro grinned at the irony. 'You didn't go to any trouble when I called on you the first time.'

She bit down on her lip and her cheeks coloured

up in the way he adored so much. 'That was different...'

He bent down to kiss her again. 'So it was.'

As they were walking back to the villa Teddy heard the roar of a sports car in the distance. She watched as the car came at breakneck speed up the long driveway towards them, the dust clouding behind the car's racing tyres in great billows. 'He's going very fast.'

'My brother only has two speeds,' Alejandro said drily. 'Fast and faster.'

The car screeched to a halt with a spray of gravel barely a metre from where they were standing. A tall dark-haired man unfolded himself with lazy grace from the vehicle. At first glance it was like looking at a carbon copy of Alejandro, but then, as Luiz got closer she could see the subtle differences. He had the same raven-black hair and were-they-black-were-they-brown? eyes with strong eyebrows and eyelashes thick and long enough to make any woman who spent a fortune on mascara weep in envy.

He was more or less the same height as Alejandro and had the same sharply chiselled jaw, which looked as if it hadn't seen a razor in at least eighteen hours. But while Alejandro's nose was long and straight, Luiz's was hawk-like, giving him a slightly more intimidating air. But to counter that his mouth looked as if it was well used to smiling, as there were laughter lines either side of it and about his intelligent eyes.

He flashed a white-toothed smile at Teddy as he offered her his hand. '*Hola*. Welcome to the family. It's nice to have a sister at last.'

'How do you do?'

Luiz's dark eyes twinkled as he unashamedly gave her the once-over. 'Not my brother's usual type but you're beautiful, for all that he said.'

'I did not say she was—'

'My brother has no sense of humour.' Luiz slung an arm around Teddy's shoulders and gave her a squeeze. 'Maybe while you're here you can help him with that.'

'Don't handle her so roughly.' Alejandro's tone was gruff, like an older man talking to a wilful child.

Luiz's brows rose but Teddy could see a mischievous twinkle in his eyes. 'I thought you said it was a paper—?'

'It's not.' Alejandro took her hand and drew her protectively to his side.

Luiz rocked back on his heels as he surveyed them both. 'Well, well, well.'

Teddy knew she was blushing like a schoolgirl but there was nothing she could do about it. The difference between the two men could never be more apparent. Alejandro was serious, steady and task oriented, reluctant to show emotion. Luiz was charming and cheeky and playful and wore his emotions proudly. But while it looked like a standoff between them, she could tell they were close.

'Quick work, bro,' Luiz said with another devilish grin. 'Can't say I blame you. Might as well make the most of the situation, especially now.'

Alejandro's brows drew together. 'Why especially now?'

Luiz's dark eyes glinted as he tossed his keys in the air and deftly caught them. 'Mamá has come to stay. She arrived this afternoon.'

Teddy looked up at Alejandro but his expression was impassive. 'So?' he said.

Luiz pocketed his keys. 'She wants to meet her daughter-in-law. I'm putting on a little party tonight so you can introduce Teddy to her.'

Alejandro's mouth was tightly set. 'I don't want her anywhere near Teddy.'

Luiz continued to study his older brother while he addressed Teddy. 'It seems you've worked a miracle, Teddy, and so quickly too. I never thought I'd see the day.'

'I mean it, Luiz.' Alejandro's tone was adamant. 'She's only here to find fault or stir up trouble. You know what she's like.'

'Don't worry,' Luiz said. 'I've invited a few others to dilute her company. It'll look strange if you don't show up. You don't have to stay long.' His dark eyes twinkled again. 'You can make up some excuse about still being on your honeymoon.'

Teddy could hear Alejandro grinding his teeth as they watched Luiz drive back down the driveway like a Formula One driver heading towards the chequered flag. 'I don't mind going to the party,' she said. 'Luiz is right. It would look strange if we didn't.'

He looked at her with a frown, his hands holding hers. 'If I could spare you one thing it would be this.'

'I'll make sure I wear my big girl pants.'

A flicker of a smile appeared at the corner of his mouth. 'I prefer you without them.'

Teddy gave him a look of mock horror. 'Not in front of your mother, surely?'

He pushed a strand of her sweaty hair back behind her ear, his expression taking on that deeply thoughtful and serious look she had come to draw such hope from. 'That's what I like about you, *mi amor*. You have courage. It's one of the values I admire most in people.'

He liked her? He admired her? Did that mean he...*loved* her? She was almost too scared to frame the thought in case her hopes were dashed before they had time to grow. 'I'm sure it will be a lovely party and a good chance to meet some of Luiz's friends. He's very charming, isn't he?'

Alejandro's serious expression relaxed into a smile. 'Yes. He knows how to work the room.

He's been like it since he was a kid. He laughs his way through life.'

'I like him.'

'I thought you might. He likes you too.'

'You think so?'

He tapped her on the end of her nose with a feather-light touch. 'How could he not?'

Teddy gazed into his eyes, struck by how warm and tender they were. Should she say something? Tell him she loved him? Or was it too soon? What if she was wrong? What if he was just acting the role for the sake of his staff? He had a business to run after all. He wouldn't want rumours of trouble at home to jeopardise things. 'Alejandro…'

'Once this party is out of the way I'm going to take you away for a couple of nights,' he said. 'Just the two of us.'

'But what about Sofi and Jorge?'

He smiled again. 'That's another thing I like about you. You're always thinking of others.'

'You do that too.'

'Occasionally, perhaps.'

'All the time,' Teddy said. 'Look at all you've

done for Luiz. And now you're doing it for Sofi and Jorge. You've put your own life on hold for them.'

He gave her another long look before taking her hand and bringing it up to his mouth. 'You've been good for them. You've done more in the short time you've been here than I have in months.'

'They're good kids.' *I'll miss them when I'm gone.* Teddy could hear the unspoken words hovering in the silence. Surely if he wanted her to stay he would say it now?

But no, he didn't.

He simply gave her one of his on-off smiles and took her hand and led her inside the villa.

CHAPTER ELEVEN

'YOU LOOK AMAZING,' Sofi said, standing back after putting the final touches to Teddy's hair and make-up. 'See? What did I tell you? I'm good at hair and make-up, *sì*?'

Teddy checked her reflection in the mirror and gasped out loud. 'You are indeed.'

It was like looking at a new version of herself—a more sophisticated, glamorous version. Her hair was swept up in a demi-chignon, the top part teased to give her hair height, the lower strands in loose waves that bobbed around her shoulders. Her make-up was understated as per her instructions, but somehow Sofi had managed to highlight the grey-blue of her eyes with the varying tones of eyeshadow and eyeliner and with the coating of mascara her lashes looked as long as spider's legs. Her mouth was shimmering with a coating of strawberry-flavoured lip-gloss that had a base colour of rose.

There was a sound at the door and Sofi put down her brushes to speak to Alejandro as he came in. '*Now* will you agree to send me to beauty college?'

He took in Teddy's appearance with a smile. 'You've done an excellent job but you had good material to work with. You might not find it so easy working with someone less beautiful.'

'He thinks I'm too young to go and live in Buenos Aires,' Sofi said to Teddy. 'Tell him I'm not. I want to be a hair and make-up artist. I want to work in the movies.'

'I told you before—I'll think about it,' Alejandro said. 'Now, get out of here before I change my mind.'

Sofi pouted as she flounced out of the room. 'You'd make a terrible father. You're too strict.'

'What do you think, *mi amor*?' Alejandro asked once the echo of the slammed door had receded. 'Would I make a terrible father?'

Teddy shivered as his hands came down on her bare shoulders as he stood behind her dressing table stool. 'I think you'd be a wonderful father. You've certainly had plenty of practice.'

His smile was a little crooked. 'I have at that. Are you nervous about tonight?'

'Not a bit.' It was a lie but she didn't want him to worry about her. He had enough on his plate to deal with, seeing his mother for the first time in years. She didn't want to add to his stress.

His hands left her shoulders as he reached into his jacket pocket. He brought out a long thin velvet jewellery case. 'I have something for you.' He opened the case and took out a fine white gold chain with a sapphire pendant set in a surround of glittering diamonds and a pair of matching earrings.

Teddy sat very still as he fastened the pendant around her neck. His fingers brushing against her skin made her think of how it had felt to have them touching her intimately. Would she ever learn to live without him if things didn't progress the way she desperately hoped they would?

She met his gaze in the mirror once she had inserted the earrings in her ear lobes. 'They're gorgeous.'

His put his hands back on her shoulders. She felt the hard warmth of him against her shoulder blades and suppressed another shiver of longing. 'You're gorgeous. I mean it, Teddy. You take my breath away.'

She put her hand over one of his. 'Thank you.'

'For stating the obvious?'

'For helping me gain confidence.'

'You did it all by yourself, *querida*.'

Teddy picked up her purse and carefully stood from the stool. She glanced at her stick leaning against the dressing table. How dearly she would have loved to walk into Luiz's party using Alejandro's arm as her only support.

Alejandro handed the stick to her, his gaze warm and supportive. 'Best to be on the safe side.'

I crossed to the dangerous side long ago, Teddy thought.

The cocktail party was in full swing by the time Teddy and Alejandro arrived. She tried to ignore the buzzing hive of nerves in her stomach as she was introduced to the other guests. She forgot most of their names almost as soon as they were introduced to her because her gaze kept going to the centre of the room where Alejandro's mother held centre stage.

Describing Eloise Beauchamp as beautiful would be an understatement even though she was well into her fifties. She was dark-haired and tall and willowy, with long legs and slim arms and a waist that was so tiny it looked as if a man's hands could span it. Elegance, sophistication and poise surrounded her like an aura. Her clothes were designer, her jewellery stunning, her hair and make-up perfect.

Teddy felt her chest fold in dismay. How was she supposed to impress a woman so perfectly turned out as that? The ache in her hip gripped her with renewed force as Alejandro led her further into the room and she almost stumbled but for the band of steel his arm provided around her. 'Careful, *querida*.'

'I'm fine.'

He interlocked his fingers with hers. 'We don't have to stay long if you—'

'I said I'm fine.' She took a glass of champagne from the waiter. 'It's been ages since I've been to a party.'

Alejandro took a glass of orange juice off the tray the waiter held. If he was tense about coming face to face with his mother there was no sign of it in his expression.

Luiz came over, leading Eloise by one of her beautifully manicured hands. Teddy curled her fingers with their bitten nails into her palm, wishing she had thought to get Sofi to glue on some fake nails.

Eloise's hazel eyes went straight to Alejandro's brown ones, her beautifully shaped lips curving in a smile that turned the temperature down three or four degrees. 'I believe congratulations are in order.'

Alejandro didn't bother with the pretence of smiling. His expression was as coldly distant as if greeting a stranger. 'I'd like you to meet my wife, Teddy. Teddy, my mother, Eloise.'

'Hello,' Teddy said. 'I'm pleased to meet you.'

Eloise ran her gaze over Teddy's figure and outfit in that quickly assessing way some women did when they were introduced to each other.

The dress she had felt so beautiful in back at the villa now felt like a chaff bag. Her ballet flat shoes felt as if she were wearing flip-flops at a formal ball. Her walking stick… Well, what could she say? The look on Eloise's face said it all. The only thing Teddy wasn't ashamed of was the jewellery Alejandro had given her. It far outshone what Eloise was wearing, but then she wondered with a sharp little pang if that was why he had given them to her.

'This is an unusual way to meet one's new daughter-in-law, is it not?' Eloise said. 'I would've come to the wedding if I'd been invited.'

And upstage the bride. Not that it would have taken much to do that, Teddy thought. 'We wanted to keep things private on account of my father's recent death.'

'My deepest sympathies on your loss.'

'Thank you.'

Eloise turned her gaze back to her oldest son. 'You haven't come to visit me in my new home in Giverny. You know you're always welcome.'

'I've been busy.'

Eloise stretched her lips into a tight smile as she faced Teddy. 'Alejandro has never forgiven me for not being perfect. He has such impossibly high standards. He was always like that, even as a young child. It was terribly tiresome.'

'Excuse me.' Alejandro gave his mother a formal nod before turning away to someone who had tapped him on the shoulder to speak to him and Luiz about the resort plans. Teddy had a feeling he would have turned away in any case. He clearly loathed any communication with his mother, who seemed to use any opportunity she could to denigrate him. It reminded her so much of her father's treatment of her.

'So, he got married after all,' Eloise continued. 'I wondered if he ever would after his fiancée left him.'

'She didn't love him.' *And I don't believe he loved her.*

'No, I imagine not.' Eloise fingered the rim of her champagne glass. 'It's a very big mistake marrying a man you don't love. It causes all sorts of heartache in the end. For everybody.'

'You didn't love Alejandro and Luiz's father?'

Eloise's sigh sent her slim shoulders down. 'No. I wasn't ready for marriage and, as it turned out, neither was I cut out for motherhood. I found it all so…claustrophobic. I know that probably sounds awfully selfish but I wanted my own life. I wanted my freedom. After Paco's accident I could see I would never have a life again if I stayed. It would be sucked away by his needs. I wasn't strong enough to stay. I knew I would end up having a breakdown or something.'

'It must have been a difficult decision to leave the boys.'

Eloise gave another one of those cool smiles. 'Everyone is so romantic about the notion of having children. But it's not for everyone. I hated being pregnant. I hated giving birth and I hated having children hanging off my skirts, dependent on me for every need.' She glanced briefly in Alejandro's direction before adding, 'And, of course, some children are much more difficult to handle than others.'

Teddy was sure it wasn't Alejandro who had been difficult. Eloise struck her as someone exactly like her father. Her needs, her wants and goals would always come before anyone else's. 'What about a nanny? Surely that would have been preferable to leaving the boys to fend for themselves?'

Eloise arched her brows in an imperious manner. 'It will be interesting to see how you cope if and when you have children. Have you thought of how you will manage, with your disability?'

Teddy stood stock-still with shock at the older woman's rudeness. How could someone as gentle and loving and protective as Alejandro have a mother who was so cold and unfeeling? 'What I lack in mobility I will make up for in love,' she said.

Alejandro reappeared by her side, his tall firm presence giving her such comfort and reassurance Teddy felt as if she could have taken on Goliath. 'Is everything all right?'

'Why wouldn't it be?' Eloise said. 'Your wife and I were just having a little chat about having children. How many are you planning on having?'

Alejandro's expression was like a mask. 'It's

not something we've discussed. We've only been married a short time.'

'Did you know Mercedes has left her husband?' Eloise said. 'What a pity you didn't wait a little longer to see if you could talk her round.'

'I'm perfectly happy with the choice I've made.'

Was he? Teddy wondered with a sinking heart. Or was he pretending to be? What sort of choice was she? She had been thrust upon him. He hadn't had any choice. And what sort of mother would she make? Eloise's words were like daggers to her heart. How *would* she cope? Why was she even asking herself the question? It wasn't as if Alejandro was suddenly going to fall in love with her. He might like her company and enjoy making love with her but that was as far as it went. She would be a fool to hope for anything more. Tonight was a confirmation of the different worlds they inhabited. Surrounded by the glamorous polo crowd she felt like a donkey at a dressage event.

Luiz came over, leading a young blonde

woman by the hand. 'We're going to dance. Want to join us?'

Alejandro's arm tightened around Teddy's waist. 'Not this time.'

Teddy watched as Luiz took to the dance floor doing a sexy tango with his partner. It was like making love while still fully clothed. There was such passion and fire in the dance of the nation.

It hit her then like a blow to the pit of her stomach. She could never be a part of Alejandro's world. She would never be able to dance like that, to be a proper partner for him on the dance floor, or in any capacity. She would always be standing on the sidelines because she was not one of the beautiful people. The disappointment was crushing. She could feel it building in her chest like a weight pressing down on her heart. She couldn't breathe. The room seemed too crowded. The music too loud.

Alejandro turned to speak to someone next to him and Teddy seized her chance to get some air. She murmured a quick, 'Excuse me,' and slipped out of his loose hold. She was halfway across the room when her stick caught on the edge of the carpet that fringed the dancing area. She tried to regain her balance but a lively couple doing the tango didn't see her and bumped her. It was only a gentle collision but it was enough to send her down. Even though the music was loud she could hear the collectively indrawn breath of everyone in the room. She felt the shocked and pitying gaze of every eye. Shame coursed through her, staining her cheeks with hot burning colour.

Alejandro was with her within a second, bending down to help her up. '*Querida*, are you all right?'

'I'm fine.' Teddy got up with as much dignity as she could but it wasn't enough. This was how it would always be. Making a fool of herself. Being clumsy and stupid and ungainly. How long would he be patient? How long before he would come to resent it, like her father had done?

She looked at the sea of faces in front of her. Eloise was looking at her with a haughty expression on her face as if she couldn't understand what her oldest son saw in his choice of bride.

Teddy gripped her stick and straightened her shoulders as she faced Alejandro. 'I want to go home.'

'But of course.'

She waited until they were outside the party room before she said, 'I mean home to England.'

Alejandro's brows came together in a frown. 'What did my mother say to you?'

She gripped her stick so tightly her palm ached. 'This is not about your mother.'

'Then what is it about?'

Teddy was trying not to cry. She didn't want to show how emotionally undone she was. She wanted to be cool and in control but somehow it wasn't as easy as it used to be. 'How can you ask that? Didn't you see what happened just then?'

'You fell over because those stupid people weren't watching where they were going,' he said, frowning even more heavily. 'I blame myself for not being with you. I got distracted by one of the local councillors who wanted to talk about something.'

'Oh, so you're going to be with me all the time in future, are you? Is that what you're planning?'

His gaze softened as he took her free hand. 'As a matter of fact, that's exactly what I'm planning. I was going to talk to you about it when we go away for a couple of days. This doesn't have to be temporary, *mi amor*. We could make it last a lifetime.'

Teddy snatched her hand back before she was tempted to believe it could work. It could never work. He would end up hating her for limiting him. For holding him back, just like all his other pressing responsibilities.

'A lifetime of what? Of you standing on the sidelines with me at every party because I can't dance? How long before you find someone else who can? How long before you find someone to do everything I can't do?'

His expression darkened. 'You're talking nonsense, Teddy. You're creating obstacles that aren't even there. You can do so much more than you realise.'

She steeled her resolve, pulling further away from him, holding onto her stick for support instead of him. 'I can't do this, Alejandro. I don't care if I lose everything. It's not worth it to see everyone pitying me or, worse, pitying *you* for marrying me.'

His jaw made a crunching sound. 'My mother is a troublemaker. I told you not to listen to her.'

'She didn't say anything to me I haven't already said to myself.'

'But that's exactly my point,' he said in accents of frustration. 'You're the one limiting yourself. We could have a good life together. I know we can.'

'You're not listening to me, Alejandro.' She eyeballed him, determined not to break. Not to give in. Not to be persuaded by him, only to have him regret it later. 'I want to leave.'

A battle went on behind his gaze. Then she saw it move over his face as each and every muscle went into a tight lockdown. His mouth was pulled almost flat, the words coming out in a flat monotone stripped of any emotion. 'All right. Leave. Go on. Do it. I won't have people saying I forced you to stay. If you want to go, then go. I'll even book your flight for you.'

'That won't be necessary.' It was ironic that

Teddy used the very same phrase he had used the day they were married. 'I can find my own way home.'

Luiz came out to where Alejandro was standing as the taxi pulled away from the front of the villa. 'Where's she going?'

'Home to pack.'

'You're letting her leave?'

'I shouldn't have made her come in the first place.'

'But I thought—?'

'We can build the resort somewhere else.' He kept his tone businesslike and steady even though he felt as if every one of his organs was being sucked down a giant sinkhole in his stomach. 'There's a good place not far from here. It's got good drainage and it's closer to the airport. We could put in an offer. See if they take it.'

Luiz frowned so darkly his brows became a single line. 'I thought you two were great together.'

Alejandro stretched his mouth into an on-off smile. 'It was an act.'

'Pretty convincing if you ask me.'

'I surprised myself.'

Luiz gave him a narrowed look. 'You sure you're not in love with her?'

He kept his expression blank. 'Whatever gave you that idea?'

'It's the first time I've seen you chill out a bit. You seemed less work obsessed.'

Alejandro gave his brother an ironic glance. 'Since when have you become the big expert on recognising love? Have you fallen for someone yourself?'

Luiz held his hands up. 'Hey, don't go jinxing me, man. I'm not claiming to know anything about it. I'm just saying you guys were good together. Like a team, you know?'

We were. Now we're not. The ache in Alejandro's chest was like a bolt being tightened to breaking point. The threads were scored raw.

'But what if she's in love with you?'

'She's not.'

'You sure?'

Alejandro looked at the tail lights of the taxi fading into the distance. 'I'm sure.'

CHAPTER TWELVE

TEDDY WAS PACKING her bag when Sofi came in without knocking. 'You can't leave,' she said. 'Alejandro won't let you.'

Teddy snapped the bag closed. 'He has let me.'

'But he loves you. I know he does.' Sofi's eyes were bright with tears. 'He's ordered hundreds of roses for the new garden. Doesn't that prove it?'

Teddy turned to pick up her passport. 'I can't stay. I'm sorry. I can't explain it. It would take too long.'

'You're not just leaving him,' Sofi said. 'You're leaving us. Jorge and me. If you didn't plan on staying, then why did you make us love you?'

There was the sound of footsteps coming along the passage and the door burst open so hard it banged against the wall. Jorge stood there with an angry expression on his young face. 'If you think I'm going to beg you to stay then think again,' he said, sounding so much like Alejandro it made her chest tighten another notch.

'I'm sorry but—'

'But what?' Jorge spat back. 'You haven't got the courage to deal with what life has dealt you? Why don't you take a look around at what other people get dealt with?'

Teddy swallowed the lump of emotion that was clogging her throat. 'This isn't easy for me...'

'So you're taking the easy way out,' Sofi chimed in. 'You're running away. You are a cow...what is the word?'

'Coward,' Jorge said with a look of disgust.

Teddy looked at their disappointed faces. Saw the love Sofi wasn't afraid to hide. Saw the love Jorge was doing his best to conceal.

Had she got it wrong?

Did Alejandro love her? Was that why he had planned to take her away for a couple of days, to tell her in private, away from all his responsibilities and distractions?

She had panicked at the party. All her old insecurities had landed on her when she'd taken that tumble. In that moment of embarrassment and shame she had discarded every bit of evidence that Alejandro cared for her. She had dismissed every possibility of a future together. Sofi was right. She had taken the coward's way out. The one thing Alejandro said he admired in her was courage and yet when it came down to the wire she had failed to demonstrate it. She should have picked herself up off that floor and laughed it off. She should have reached for Alejandro's hand and asked him to dance with her, even if she couldn't do it as well as she would like. It wouldn't be perfect but it would be good enough.

She was good enough.

Hadn't he been proving that for the whole time they were married?

There was the sound of more footsteps coming along the corridor and Teddy looked towards the door to see Alejandro standing there with a stern expression. 'What are you two doing up here?' he said to Sofi and Jorge.

'You have to convince her to stay!' Sofi said.

'I wouldn't bother.' Jorge scowled.

Alejandro jerked his head towards the door. 'Out.'

'Not until you beg her to stay,' Sofi said.

'He doesn't need to do that,' Teddy said, meeting his gaze. 'I've changed my mind.'

Nothing changed in his stern expression but she saw him take a deep swallow. 'Why?'

'Because I love you.'

His eyes lost their distant hardness. He swallowed again. Twice. 'I love you too. I should have told you earlier. I wanted to, down at the stables this afternoon, but—'

'I knew it!' Sofi said, and high-fived Jorge, who was trying to hide a smile.

Alejandro rolled his eyes and turned to them both. 'Do you mind? I'd like a little bit of privacy here.'

Sofi clasped her hands together as if she was watching a romantic movie coming to an end. Jorge went back to pretending he was bored. Teddy was so full of love for them she was sure she was going to burst.

But then Jorge grabbed Sofi by the arm on his

way to the door. 'Better get out of here before they start kissing.'

Sofi dragged her feet. 'I can't leave *now*. This is the best bit.'

Alejandro pointed to the door and, after a long theatrical sigh and a mutter about what a horrible spoilsport he was, blah, blah, blah, Sofi grudgingly left with Jorge, snipping the door shut behind her.

Alejandro brought Teddy close with a grin. 'Do you really want to take on those two unruly brats as well as me?'

Teddy put her arms around him and hugged him tightly. 'I can't think of anything nicer. We can be a family. It's what I've always wanted.'

He looked down at her with a more serious expression. 'I thought I was going to lose you. I can't believe I was so stupid back at the party. I was too proud to stop you leaving.'

'You really love me? Really and truly?'

His gaze was so tender it made her heart swell until her chest cavity felt too small. 'I think I fell in love with you that first day. You looked so proud and defiant, dressed like a bag lady and glaring at me as if I'd climbed out of a primeval swamp.'

Teddy touched his face with her hand, barely able to believe her dream was coming to life in front of her eyes. 'I'm not sure when I fell in love with you. It sort of crept up on me. I was so determined to hate you but you kept surprising me with your kindness and gentleness.'

He put his hand over hers, holding it to his face. 'You're the best thing that's ever happened to me. I think I've only been half alive until you came into my life. Marry me, Teddy.'

She gave him a puzzled look. 'But we're already married.'

'Not the way you wanted to be.' He stroked her hair. 'Not the way you deserve to be.'

She gave him a teasing smile. 'Can I have roses?'

His eyes glinted. 'Hundreds of them. Thousands. Millions, even.'

Teddy had a sudden thought and frowned. 'But what am I going to tell Audrey and Henry? And what will I do with Marlstone Manor?'

'I've always fancied an English retreat. The

manor would make a great polo breeding estate. We could split our time between the two countries. That way, we could get the best of the weather.'

'Do you really mean it?'

'There's one thing you need to learn when handling a Valquez man. Once we make up our mind on something we never back down.'

She sent him a twinkling look. 'I would call that arrogance.'

His eyes smouldered as they held hers. 'Then maybe you'll have to tame me. Are you up to the task?'

'When shall I start?'

Alejandro brought his mouth down to her beaming one. 'No time like the present.'

* * * * *